W9-AUI-751

Killing Cousins

by the same author

Enter Second Murderer
Blood Line
Deadly Beloved

Killing Cousins

An Inspector Faro Mystery

Alanna Knight

St. Martin's Press
New York

For information, address St. Martin's Press, 175 Fifth Avenue, New York, N.Y. 10010.

Library of Congress Cataloging-in-Publication Data

Knight, Alanna.
Killing cousins : an Inspector Faro mystery / Alanna Knight.
p. cm.
"A Thomas Dunne book."
ISBN 0-312-07008-X
I. Title.
PR6061.N45K55 1992
823'.914—dc20 91-34917
CIP

First published in Great Britain by Macmillan London Limited.

First U.S. Edition: January 1992
10 9 8 7 6 5 4 3 2 1

For Agnes

Killing Cousins

Chapter One

There was nothing in the least sinister about the day that began it all. In the gardens beyond the windows of 9 Sheridan Place, late roses bloomed.

A morning haze of sunshine shimmering on Arthur's Seat promised another day unusually warm for that early autumn of 1871 and criminals were singularly inactive in the annals of the Edinburgh City Police.

What had happened to crime? Was he witnessing the dawn of a new age? Such were Detective Inspector Jeremy Faro's musings, indulging in his second cup of Earl Grey tea, as the housekeeper Mrs Brook set down the morning mail.

Across the table, Dr Vincent Beaumarcher Laurie tore open his solitary letter. 'By all that's wonderful. Amazing!'

Such sentiments brought the merest twitch of an eyebrow from his stepfather's direction. Used to Vince's extravagant reactions to quite trivial domestic situations, Faro dismissed such exuberance as a necessary outlet to the more sombre expectations of a young man about to set up as a general practitioner in medicine.

'This is quite astonishing, Stepfather,' and Vince waved the letter before him.

As Faro's own mail was at once recognisable as a dreary selection of tradesmen's bills and an ill-written abusive epistle full of rude words from one of the criminal fraternity anxious to remain anonymous, he vastly preferred to be astonished by whatever his stepson was about to reveal.

Especially as his remaining letter also bore an Orkney postmark. From his mother. He had left it unopened until he had been rightly fortified with a third cup of tea. Its contents, he did not doubt, would contain the usual gentle reproaches about his neglect of his two motherless children.

'This is from Francis Balfray, Stepfather,' said Vince. 'I don't suppose you remember Francis?'

Faro bristled slightly. If there was one thing on which he prided himself it was his excellent memory. 'I do indeed. The golden lad. Three years ahead of you. Claimed acquaintance through some remote Orcadian link. And you never liked him in the least as I recall. Priggish, wasn't that how you dismissed him?'

As he spoke, Faro's mind presented a vivid picture of a slightly built handsome youth, reputedly a brilliant student, the joy of his tutors.

'That's amazingly perceptive of you, Stepfather, considering you only met him for a few minutes.'

'I further recall that he was, despite his somewhat effeminate appearance, which might have brought grave doubts, engaged to be married.'

As Vince ran a hand through bright curls that not even his worst enemies could have considered suspect after his performance on the rugby field and within my lady's chamber, Faro wondered if Balfray's conscientious devotion to his studies was perhaps the main reason why Vince and his boon companions, Rob and Walter, found Balfray's company somewhat tedious.

'I recall that his betrothed was an Orkney cousin, a childhood sweetheart. Am I right?'

'You are indeed, Stepfather. And marry her he did.' Vince picked up the letter again. 'That's what this is all about. Poor Thora has been taken mysteriously ill over the last few months. Sounds as if she has fallen foul of the local speywife.' He looked across at Faro. 'Been ill-wished, or something.'

At his stepfather's ill-concealed grunt of disbelief, Vince continued hastily. 'That's what he says. Listen to this: "I know it's all superstitious rubbish, but you have no idea what the island is like or the kind of people I'm dealing with. For the life of me, I can't discover what ails my dear wife. I've tried every kind of diagnosis and, without a second opinion, I'm in a devil of a fix. If I can't get help I feel something dreadful is about to happen – and soon. But my wife refuses to let me call in another doctor from the mainland. I'm desperate, Vince old chap, otherwise I wouldn't dream of burdening you with my problems. However, I have been prevailed upon to approach you by your dear grandmother, Mrs Faro— " '

Vince was momentarily interrupted by a stifled groan from his stepfather. He continued: ' "Mrs Faro is our dear good friend and urges me to write to you without further delay. She has been wonderful to poor Thora during her illness and has the highest regard for your capabilities. I'd look upon it as the greatest possible favour, old chap, if you could spare the time . . . " '

Vince looked across the table. 'Well, what do you think of that?'

Faro was already tearing open his mother's letter. ' "Dearest Jeremy, As you'll notice from the address above, I have taken on the post of housekeeper at Balfray Castle. It was advertised a few weeks ago. There were few replies, no one suitable— " '

'I'm not surprised, Stepfather. From what Francis told me, Balfray is both small and remote. Can't understand why he was so wild about it. As for Grandma marooning herself there . . . '

'May I continue?' asked Faro. ' "The post is only

for the summer months to help out until poor Thora recovers her strength. After all, we are distantly related on your poor dear father's side of the family and Rose and Emily so enjoy the special thrill of living in a castle. The Balfrays adore them, especially as their marriage has been sadly childless." '

Faro paused to fortify himself with another sip of tea. 'Where was I? Oh yes. This is where you come in: "Dear Vince will have heard from Dr Francis. I assure you he is almost out of his mind with anxiety, suffering as much as poor Thora, who seems to be fading away before our eyes. I have no doubt that Vince will rally to the call and be eager to help his old friend in any way he can . . ." '

Faro threw down the letter. Without any claim to psychic powers, he could guess how bad things must be. His mother's use of the prefix 'poor' was ominous in the extreme. It usually indicated those deceased or very shortly to be so.

He gave a sigh of exasperation. Although most of the time he loved his mother dearly, since no one could deny the heart of gold and the good intentions, the fact remained that she could be a sore trial, a well-meaning busybody, always ready and eager to tell everyone – her son included, first and foremost – how to run their lives.

' "Of course, if you could see your way to coming on a short visit at the same time . . ." '

Reading his expression, Vince smiled. 'Trust Grandma never to miss a trick. Very convenient to kill two birds with one stone, eh?' He folded Francis Balfray's letter carefully and, frowning, tapped his fingers on the table. 'I do think I should go, Stepfather. I've no excuse not to, really, since I'm between locums just now. And why don't you come with me? Grandma's idea isn't a bad one at that. Besides, you're always talking about going to Orkney, seeing Rose and Emily.'

Talking, yes. Talking was easy, thought Faro guiltily. There wasn't a lot of effort needed in talking without serious intent of carrying out a family visit. And yet he was tempted. Through the window, down a tree-lined road, lay the foothills of the Pentland Hills. Beyond their gentle undulating slopes, a vast open countryside beckoned, where larks still sang into a cloudless sky above a harvest newly gathered in and hedgerows bloomed, fragrant with meadowsweet.

Suddenly an escape from the sordid petty crime and grime of Edinburgh's High Street was vastly appealing.

Suspecting, by his stepfather's wistful expression, that he was weakening, Vince continued sternly, 'You deserve a holiday, Stepfather. You've had rather too many colds and stomach upsets lately. What you need is some good fresh Orkney air and Grandma's cooking.'

And, wryly saluting his absent mother's triumph, Faro smiled. Why not accompany Vince, just to appease his wretched conscience which attacked him unmercifully on his shortcomings as a father to Rose and Emily? 'Very well. We'll leave directly. Just give me time to make arrangements at the Central Office.'

But here, alas, fate stepped in. For the past year, the bane of Faro's life had been a crook, allegedly scion of an aristocratic family, whose clever frauds bore the signature *noblesse oblige*, roughly translated as 'privilege entails responsibility'.

But responsibility for what, demanded Inspector Faro? Nicknamed Lord Nob by Edinburgh City policemen exasperated by his cunning, he worked with an accomplice, a clever woman or a young man who could assume, with considerable ease, the role of either sex. Indeed, the pair were so adept at disguises Faro strongly suspected that Lord Nob had been an actor at some stage in his career.

Earlier that summer came the break that all policemen long for. An informer in the criminal fraternity, who preferred to be anonymous, had come forward with reliable information that Noblesse Oblige was to be found frequently in Aberdeen.

The local police had made little progress and Superintendent McIntosh called Faro into his office.

'I'm certain that our informer is a woman. In all probability a prostitute. One he's forgotten to pay or otherwise betrayed. How about it? This is your chance to corner Noblesse Oblige.'

It seemed too great a challenge to miss, but Faro shook his head. 'I'd go gladly, sir, but as you know, it's out of my territory. Besides, I'm about to go to Orkney for a few days' holiday.'

'You can do both – Aberdeen's your right direction.' The Superintendent flourished a letter. 'Your fame's well spread, and they've made a direct appeal to me to release you.'

Faro needed no second bidding and a disappointed Vince took ship for Orkney alone.

A week later, however, a very angry and disgruntled Inspector Faro paced the quayside at Aberdeen harbour where, once again, the hunt for his quarry had ended. The trail blazed so hopefully was lost. Once again Noblesse Oblige had outwitted his pursuers.

Faro knew when he was defeated and further pursuit a waste of time and effort. His quarry could have taken ship for a dozen different ports from Aberdeen. Heading in the direction of the shipping office for a berth back to Edinburgh's port of Leith, he noticed the Orkney boat moored at the quayside. For a moment he regarded it, frowning. Then, taking a coin from his pocket, he flipped it.

An hour later he was sailing north, bound for Kirkwall, where the rough breeze and accompanying spray cleared his head but did nothing for his digestion. A few sea miles further out found him glad to retreat into the cabin below, where the onset of night and gale force winds had him cursing his own folly.

He thought longingly of Edinburgh and his own comfortable bed as, retiring to his bunk, he lay sleepless while creaking timbers and heaving seas suggested that he had been rash indeed to anticipate a pleasant holiday in the land of his birth.

The night and his distress seemed endless but at last daylight broke upon a leaden sea and found him gloomily contemplating worse in store than bad weather. From long experience, he knew that he had but to set foot on Orkney to be irritated by his well-meaning mother with her eternal fussing. And irritation once begun tended to increase with the knowledge that the islanders were being dragged kicking and screaming into the nineteenth century.

Oblivious of scientific progress they remained happily ensconced in the Middle Ages. No marvels of machinery for them. They were content, even considering it a virtue, to live and die in smoky hovels, merely because that was the way of life of their fathers and grandfathers before them.

Rising from his uncomfortable pallet, he lit a pipe and prepared himself for his two daughters' onslaught upon his emotions and those feelings of neglect which he sought to assuage by lavishing expensive gifts on them. Gifts, alas, which were the choice of Mrs Brook, his housekeeper and left him guiltily aware of his own neglect.

He was also certain that after a polite reception and a loving letter, all were relegated to a seldom-opened cupboard, to join a regiment of dolls entirely unwanted or dresses entirely unsuitable. Their only emergence was at the annual spring clean when they were graciously donated to one of his mother's innumerable charities and good causes.

He ought to remarry. He knew that perfectly well. The girls needed a mother, as their grandmother and Mrs Brook were never weary of reminding him. Only once since Lizzie's death had he met anyone he would have cared to spend the rest of his life with, but fate had decreed otherwise, both confirming and gratifying his own opinion that he was doomed to remain a widower.

An unexpected sparkle of sunlight fanned the sea with bright diamonds and momentarily raised his spirits. But, as the ship slid into Kirkwall harbour, the clouds regathered ominously, leaving a sorry welcome of rain-dark streets and tight-packed iron-grey houses.

At the shipping office, enquiring for Balfray and fearing the worst, the clerk beamed on him. 'You're in luck, sir. Old Jamie is at this moment collecting parcels and supplies. He'll be heading for Balfray first. And I dare say he'll be glad to have a passenger.'

As the tiny rowing boat strained against the tide, Faro felt that 'glad' was something of an exaggeration since his companion was of a taciturn disposition, acknowledging his presence with the briefest nod.

Faro, however, soon had problems more pressing than popularity to dwell upon. Only by a valiant struggle to occupy his mind with an intense concentration on his own boots could he manage to retain his breakfast. All around them a wildly seesawing horizon bestowed upon passing islands the interesting ghost shapes and sea-sprayed outlines reminiscent, in a more imaginative man, of basking whales. In a sea world of charcoal grey against a sky only several shades paler, the short crossing seemed endless.

Passing close by a tiny island inhabited by a seal colony, the occupants turned in their direction faces curiously human and bearing remarkably more expression than the stolid boatman.

'Hullo there!' Faro's wave and his cheery greeting caused a flicker of alarm and astonishment in his dour companion. It clearly indicated misgivings that he had a madman aboard who laughed out loud as the seals stared back, mildly indignant, like haughty and outraged old gentlemen. Who could doubt that such resemblance had given rise to legends of mermaids and seal people? Faro smiled, remembering the child he had once been, when he had believed in such myths and begged his parents for more. But not in Edinburgh. There he preferred not to remember what was patent absurdity.

Through the spray, an island larger than the rest loomed hopefully. Yes, those tall turrets visible through the twisted shapes of trees must be Balfray Castle. High above the tiny landing stage, the sea-bitten outline of one wall was all that remained of the original castle.

His sudden decision had left no time to alert Vince to his arrival and now, as landfall approached, he wondered anxiously whether Vince had managed to avert disaster and produce some miracle cure for Thora Balfray.

Returning his attention to the headland, he saw an unlovely squat building with a bell tower. The church which had arisen recently from the disused castle's purloined stone, no doubt, but lacking a spire. Such embellishments were prudently omitted from these gale-tossed islands.

His eye travelled upward to where, perched perilously and alarmingly insecure, stood one wall of an old priory and a kirkyard, whose ancient tombstones leaned at mad angles and tumbled in a rickety progress to the very edge of the steep cliffs.

'Aye, there's one body whose head'll no be sore this night,' was the boatman's first laconic comment since they had started out.

Following the direction of the pointing finger, Faro observed the tiny black shapes of a trail of mourners.

'You'll have just missed the funeral, man,' the boatman added with a shake of his head. A certain relish of tone hinted that this was a matter of infinite regret.

Then waxing voluble, 'Won't be many more up there. Hear tell the laird intends closing up the kirkyard and the family vault. Sea's eating away the cliff. Not enough soil there to keep the dead decently in their graves. Bones always falling on to the rocks and being washed away. Hands and feet and all. Rings on her fingers and bells on her toes, like the old rhyme says,' he added with a chuckle of unmistakably gruesome delight.

Shading his eyes against the sea-spray, Faro studied the tiny band of mourners and, with a growing dread, asked the name of the deceased.

'Nay, I dinnae know who it might be,' was the reply.

As the boatman threw all his efforts into steering them towards the shore, Faro discovered that landing was a matter of launching oneself forward at that brief instant when boat and quayside met. Choosing the right moment was imperative, the penalty for mistiming a very uncomfortable drenching, and Faro felt inordinately proud of his achievement in 'stepping ashore' as it was called, dry and clutching his luggage.

Indecisive for a moment, he hovered, about to head in the general direction of the castle's ornate gates.

'Stepfather . . . wait . . . wait!'

Vince was hurrying down the cliff road to greet him.

'I thought it was you, Stepfather. You did get my telegraph about Thora then?' And, without waiting for a reply, he said, 'I'm here to collect a box from Aberdeen.' And to the boatman, 'Have you something for Dr Laurie? Ah yes, that's it.'

And, acknowledging the small wooden box placed in his hands, he said, 'Come along, Stepfather. How clever of you to arrive at exactly the right time,' and set off along the road at a jaunty pace.

'What about Thora Balfray?'

'As I told you, she died last week. Poor Thora. It was in the wire I sent to you at Sheridan Place.'

'I haven't been home, Vince. I've been trailing Noblesse Oblige all over Aberdeen. A thoroughly abortive pastime, I might add.'

'What rotten luck,' Vince sighed sympathetically. 'Even if you had been at home, I've discovered that the word urgent means nothing here, so I doubt whether you would have got my message. Anyway, I'm delighted to see you and I can hardly wait to see Grandma's face when you walk in.'

'Rose and Emily?'

Vince shook his head. 'Staying in Kirkwall now that school has started. Grandma only has them for the weekends. They love that, I hear. Enchanted by living in a real castle, every little girl's dream come true.'

'It can't be a very happy place just now.'

'True,' said Vince, frowning at the tree-lined horizon.

'Tell me, how are my wee lasses?' Faro's smile was tender.

'Not wee – peedie's the word. You'll have to get used to that in Orkney. Oh, they're in splendid spirits.' And Vince warmed to this change of subject. 'And Grandma too. There's nothing like a funeral to bring out the best in her. The life and soul of this whole wretched business. Organising everyone. I don't know how Thora would have ever got kisted without her.'

Faro looked at him sharply. Vince's humour tended towards the macabre.

'I mean it, Stepfather. Francis is utterly devastated. Just like a dazed child. Locked himself in his room. Went to pieces completely.' Vince sighed. 'You can pay your respects to the poor chap at the funeral wake. I've made arrangements for you to stay at the castle, by the way.'

'Is there room for me?'

Vince laughed. 'There are about thirty bedrooms, so you can take your pick. And I'll find you a nice black cravat for the wake. All you need. You needn't appear unless you want to, of course, but it would be considered a mark of respect.'

At his stepfather's questioning look, he added, 'It's traditional when one of the laird's family dies for the whole island to be invited to the castle to speed the deceased on their way with oatcakes and drams. That,' he continued soberly, 'can take rather a long time and I gather no one is sober enough to be in charge of a boat back to the mainland for several days afterwards. Here, let me carry that.'

There followed a slight argument over who should carry Faro's luggage.

'It isn't heavy,' Faro protested.

'Heavy enough,' said Vince. 'Transporting the Immortal Bard as usual, are we?'

Faro laughed. 'My favourite travelling companion, present company excepted,' he added with a grin.

'I should have imagined you knew most of the plays by heart, Stepfather.'

But behind Vince's gentle mockery was remembrance that *The Complete Works of William Shakespeare* had been his mother's last present to his stepfather on his birthday, just weeks before she died. Since then he had carried it everywhere with him, sad memento of a happy marriage and dear Lizzie herself.

'Please yourself, Stepfather, but it's a longish walk,' said Vince, tucking the small wooden box under his arm.

At the lodge gates, he shook his head. 'No, not straight up the drive. If you aren't too tired.'

Faro's blunt reception of this concern for his well-being was in keeping with his refusal to be pampered by his doctor stepson.

'Good,' said Vince and led the way up the steep cliff path. On the rocks far below and in the shallows offshore the seals barked like maddened dogs.

Faro paused and looked down. 'I'd swear they were keeping pace with us. It's really quite uncanny.'

'They always behave like that at this time of year, or so I'm told.'

'Of course,' said Faro. 'This is St Ola's Summer.'

'Quite. When they remember the saint who lived as a hermit on Balfray. That is the Christian interpretation. There are others.'

Faro laughed. 'In pagan days, they used to believe that this was when the seal king returned to his kingdom under the waves, with a mortal bride. A grand finale to his quest, after having taken human shape and lived with men at Lammastide.'

'Used to believe, did you say? Let me tell you that they still believe every word of it. They all do lip-service to Christianity of course, but you couldn't get any lass to walk along these cliffs alone after dark, not for a handsome prince or a purse of golden guineas.'

At his stepfather's disbelieving glance, Vince added firmly, 'I mean it.'

Faro shook his head. 'Some people will believe anything.'

Such beliefs he regarded as yet another part of the islands' refusal to enter the nineteenth century. The kind of ignorance and superstition which had sent him hurrying away to make a life in Edinburgh twenty years ago.

As they entered the sea walk which separated them from the castle Faro marvelled at the stretch of trees, an extension of those he had observed clustered round the castle as the boat approached. Their gnarled appearance gave testimony to an uneasy grip on life, as they fought for survival against the elements, clinging together, huddling in tight groups against the autumn winds which yearly stripped the new growth and kept them permanently stunted.

A leafy tunnel emerged into an arbour where a former Balfray laird had thoughtfully provided stone seats. The addition of a quartet of contemplative Greek statues established the illusion of a restful sheltered spot. Here the ladies from the castle might exercise their dogs and children on winter days, the cambered walk protecting the hems of their dresses from contamination by the never-absent damp.

'Let's sit here, shall we?'

'Splendid idea,' said Faro, lighting his pipe.

Vince watched this operation in silence. 'I need a breather before we face Francis again – and the house of mourning. At least Grandma will be so surprised, and delighted, to see you.'

Faro winced at the prospect of his mother's delight which would include a refusal to allow him to do anything for himself, or admit the possibility that he might also be competent to think for himself.

When she was not persuading him that he was, like all men without a woman in their lives, utterly helpless, she indulged in an unending tide of gossip. This mainly concerned people her son had never heard of, nor, on the strength of their entire life histories, had any wish for further acquaintance.

Once again Vince glanced cautiously over his shoulder. 'We can be quite private here. I have rather a lot to tell you, Stepfather, before we reach the others. This is the one place where I suspect we won't be overlooked or overheard.'

'For heaven's sake, lad, you're being very mysterious.

Overlooked indeed. I thought I was the policeman in the family.'

There was no answering smile from his stepson who merely nodded, frowning. 'I must say I'm heartily glad to see you here. I was in the devil of a fix. Have been ever since Thora died. You see, I was certain from almost the moment I examined her that she wasn't suffering from a wasting illness.'

Pausing, he drew a deep breath and added in a whisper, 'I have every reason to believe she was poisoned.'

Chapter Two

'Thora Balfray showed definite symptoms of arsenic poisoning,' said Vince.

Faro whistled. 'Arsenic? Are you sure?'

'So sure, Stepfather, that I decided to do the Marsh Test.' Vince tapped the wooden box lying on the seat between them. 'Fortunately the apparatus is both portable and inconspicuous. The quickest way was to have it sent up from medical suppliers in Aberdeen.'

'Let us hope Francis Balfray doesn't find out.'

'I don't think he has the slightest idea. The doses must have been given in minute quantities over some considerable time and by someone very close to her,' Vince added grimly. 'No wonder poor Francis was baffled. He would be the last person in the world to think any member of his household was capable of such wickedness.'

Faro looked at him sharply. Surely the lad couldn't be that naïve? 'It has always been my experience in poisoning cases, as you know, to look first at those closest to the deceased, those who might have the most likely motive and opportunity.'

'Not so in Francis' case, Stepfather,' said Vince firmly. 'He's such an honourable fair-minded chap himself.' Observing Faro's doubtful expression, he repeated, 'I am in a devil of a fix, I can tell you. Dammit, I signed the death certificate as natural causes.'

'With your suspicions, lad? What had come over you? You know what you've done, don't you?' Faro demanded angrily. 'You've put your whole professional reputation in jeopardy.'

'Be reasonable, Stepfather, what else could I do with the distraught husband, who also happens to be a friend and a colleague, looking over my shoulder? If I'd even hinted my suspicions, I'd have had another corpse to deal with – and by his own hand. He adored Thora.'

'If you are right then, and Thora Balfray was poisoned, you'll have to summon the Procurator Fiscal from Kirkwall.'

'That is my intention. You can imagine in these circumstances how delighted I was to see you arrive on Balfray. You have so much more experience in these matters, Stepfather. I feel I can leave it all in your reliable hands.'

'It's going to create a fine stir among the islanders, isn't it?'

'I'm afraid so. In a small community like Balfray practically everyone is related, either directly by blood or by marriage.'

'And, having pulled down a hornet's nest about our heads, we'll have to keep everyone here, make sure no one leaves until the Fiscal arrives,' said Faro grimly.

Vince smiled. 'I'm glad you said we, Stepfather. Because by the time he makes his report and issues an exhumation order, I am quite certain that we will have solved the crime.'

'I shouldn't be too sure about that,' was the reply. 'Murder investigations among people related to one another can be baffling in the extreme. Relatives can be either nervous, or, knowing too much, reluctant to give information about loved ones. Alibis, I have found in such cases, are as thick on the ground as autumn leaves.'

He paused and added, 'The best that we can hope for, Vince, is that the Marsh Test proves your suspicions were unfounded.'

'Proves that I'm the over-enthusiastic over-conscientious young medic, is that it?' demanded Vince indignantly. 'Is that what you're hinting at? That too many encounters with poisonings by arsenic in the police-surgeon's laboratory have made me unnaturally suspicious? I can assure you—'

Faro put a hand on his arm. 'There, there, lad. I take your word for it, that you had just cause for suspicions. What we need to know is who had direct access to Mrs Balfray, the family and retainers, in fact.'

'That won't take long,' said Vince. 'Balfray Castle has long been on short commons. Francis, with the help of a ghillie and some workers, ran the estate until Thora's illness, then Captain Gibb, ex-Navy, distantly related, took over the factoring in return for a house on the estate.

'There's Norma, Thora's stepsister, who is betrothed to the Balfray chaplain, Reverend John Erlandson – and that completes the family.' He gave his stepfather a stern look. 'I hardly think any of them could be included as suspects.'

'What about staff?'

'Precious few. One wing of the castle is closed off since it was seldom used and the twenty servants of the last laird, Sir Joseph Balfray, were reduced to three indoors, a housekeeper and two maids, and a stable boy who doubles as handyman. Your mother will no doubt be in possession of full family histories of all of them by now.'

At Faro's wry smile, he continued, 'As for those with constant access to her food . . . '

Faro held up his hand. 'No. I don't want to know. Not at this stage, if you please. Let us wait until you've proved the test positive.'

'But all these people are unknown to you.'

Faro nodded. 'I agree. Let us just say that I have

known too many cases in the past of policemen tailoring the crime to fit a favourite suspect. I don't want to be guilty of that. If Mrs Balfray has been poisoned without any shadow of doubt, then, and then only, will be the time to consider suspects with motive and opportunity. And to reach my own conclusions.'

'We can know for certain in half an hour, Stepfather. Just as long as it takes to set up this apparatus behind the locked door of my bedroom,' said Vince grimly, picking up the wooden box and holding it like some precious gift, on his knees.

Despite his own misgivings and his hopes that Vince would be proved wrong in his suspicions, Faro was well aware of the infallibility of the Marsh Test. In constant use by police laboratories for the past forty years, it was capable of converting arsenic in body fluids and tissues into arsine gas by a simple apparatus so sensitive it could detect three-thousandths of a grain of arsenic.

'What will you use – from the deceased, I mean?'

'I kept a urine sample, that was the easiest to obtain. And some hair roots, for a double check.' Vince stood up. 'Well, shall we go?'

Leaving the sheltered arbour they almost cannoned into a man who appeared, book in hand, with surprising alacrity from behind the hedge. Of indeterminate age, his heavy beard and hair, luxuriant and dark, were at youthful variance with a somewhat ravished and deeply lined countenance, with the suspiciously florid complexion of the heavy drinker. He bowed gravely to Vince.

'Captain Gibb. This is my stepfather, Mr Faro.'

The Captain murmured a greeting and hovered indecisively.

'Are you returning to the castle with us?' asked Vince politely but, as Gibb declined the invitation and with a non-committal grunt resumed his walk down the path, Faro detected relief in Vince's response.

'I trust you have no objections to being introduced informally, Stepfather.'

'Not at all. Mr Faro sounds impressively off-duty,' was the reply, although Faro suspected that his mother must have already told everyone in Balfray the entire life story of her detective inspector son.

'As I told you, Captain Gibb is related, a remote cousin on the distaff side, or so he tells me with rather constant repetition. According to Francis, he arrived a few months ago, recently retired from active service, anxious to meet the family and write a history of the Balfrays.'

'He didn't strike me as being eager for our society.'

Vince shook his head. 'Oh, he is quite anti-social. Devotes scant time and attention to the living members of the family. They would have to be dead for at least two hundred years to engage his interest and enthusiasm. I've hardly seen him at all, but I gather that isn't unusual. When he isn't closeted in the library poring over old documents, he's to be found in Kirkwall or Stromness consulting dusty old records.'

'Has he found anything of interest?'

'Francis tells me he has made some remarkable finds, hardly world-shaking to the visitor but of breathless fascination to the Balfrays.'

Faro suppressed a smile. Vince's resistance to history was well known. He could well imagine his stepson's ill-concealed boredom regarding the Captain's activities.

'And you don't care for him, do you?'

Vince shook his head. 'Not a lot, Stepfather. He's something of a charlatan, I suspect. The archetypal sponger, preying on affluent relatives. But Francis is far too much of a gentleman to voice his opinions. As long as the Captain can feed him titbits of family history, he is sure of a berth at Balfray.'

'What has he discovered so far?'

The Balfrays boast a connection with the wicked Stuart Earls of Orkney and a dubious bastard ancestorship . . . '

'As do most of the isles, including our own family,' said Faro cynically. 'Hardly surprising considering that Earl Robert and his seven sons helped to populate the island with their many bastards.'

'Does it not amaze you how bastardy gains immediate respectability when the blood Royal is involved?' said Vince bitterly.

Faro gave him a sympathetic glance, wondering if a day would ever come when the lad's own illegitimacy ceased to plague him. His mother, Faro's dead wife, had borne him when she was a servant girl of fifteen, the result of rape in a stately home.

'This discreditable story, however, concerns the Earl of Bothwell who, despite his marriage and apparent devotion to the Queen of Scots, and being on the run after the disaster of Carberry Hill, managed to beget a bastard son during his brief and fateful visit to the island where he took refuge out of range of the guns of Kirkwall Castle.

'He slipped out and with his treasure ship headed for sanctuary in Norway, which was again denied him. According to the Balfray legend, the treasure ship and her captain gave their pursuers the slip and returned to Balfray. He brought up Bothwell's child and used the gold that had been intended to set the Queen of Scots free to establish the Balfray dynasty.'

'Remarkable!'

Vince gave him a quick look. 'And you don't believe a word of it?'

Faro smiled. 'It's an attractive story, but I suspect

highly coloured. Eminently suitable material for one of Sir Walter Scott's romances.'

'Not according to Captain Gibb. He gets very animated on the subject, insisting that he can prove it. That it's all there in the sixteenth-century documents discovered behind the wainscoting when the old castle was demolished by Francis' grandfather, who built the present building.'

Looking back in the direction which the Captain had taken, Vince added anxiously, 'Was he really walking and reading? He appeared with alarming promptitude, don't you think?'

'I was wondering the same thing myself. He could have been listening to our conversation.'

'That will give him a perfect chance to get his alibi together.'

'If he's guilty.' Faro paused and looked at Vince. 'Tell me frankly, do you have any reason to suspect that he might have poisoned Mrs Balfray?'

'Nothing direct,' said Vince regretfully.

Faro smiled. 'But you could find something, if you put your mind to it, I presume,' he added with a chiding shake of the head.

Their emergence from the shelter of the tree plunged them straight into the full face of an approaching storm.

'Is this the quick way to the castle?' Faro gasped, dragging up his coat collar and exclaiming in alarm as their path wound perilously close to the edge of the cliff.

'Watch your step, Stepfather. As you'll see, the kirkyard wall has already crumbled and fallen into the sea.' He pointed to a rubble of stones. 'Over there. That's the Dwarfie Ha'. A prehistoric settlement – Stone Age – or so I'm told.'

'Dwarfie Ha' – strange name,' said Faro, pausing for a closer look.

Vince laughed. 'No one knows what it was called originally. It's always been the Dwarfie Ha' because of the size of the rooms and their height. Where there was any roof left, a stone slab, less than four feet high, confirmed old legends that the first creatures who inhabited these islands before man were supernatural beings, trolls or hogben. And, since even to utter their names could bring disaster, they were referred to as the dwarfie folk.'

Faro walked to the edge of the neatly regulated stone maze of tiny rooms.

'Isn't it marvellous? Each with its stone cupboard, bed annexe and fireplace.'

'Amazing. How were they discovered?'

'Oh, a great storm during the last century washed the topsoil away. The subsequent excavations unearthed cooking pots, jewellery and even strings of broken beads, just as their occupants left them thousands of years ago, as if the people had fled in a great panic.'

Faro shaded his eyes, looking toward the horizon once almost continuously occupied by dragon-headed Viking ships in search of plunder and women to breed more warriors. 'An invader from the sea, do you think?'

Vince smiled impishly. 'Possibly some of your own ancestors chased them away, if looks have anything to do with it. And all you need for the part is a horned helmet, Stepfather.'

Faro's smiling glance changed into a long-suffering sigh. Vince was riding his favourite hobby-horse again.

'Have a good look at the Dwarfie Ha' before you leave,' Vince continued. 'Probably your last chance. The cliff erosion is chewing away a few feet every year now, so unless its progress can be halted it's doomed to tumble over the cliff into oblivion any day now, I'm afraid.'

As they entered the kirkyard, tombstones leaned dangerously in the direction of the cliff edge and wreaths of flowers marked the melancholy site of Thora Balfray's recent interment.

Near the Balfray vault Vince pointed to a large flat stone obviously of great antiquity. 'Another valuable artefact. According to Francis this once marked the centre, the place of sacrifice, of a prehistoric stone circle. The rest I presume has vanished into the sea long ago.'

Running a finger over the crude tree branches cut deep into the stone which led to a circular hole at the base of its trunk, he said, 'Interesting carvings, amazing how they've survived wind and weather. The Odin Stone, Stepfather. You must have heard of it?'

'Ah yes. I was brought to see it once, long ago, when I was a small child. I could have been no more than three when my father told me its grisly history, that the hole was reputedly to catch the victim's blood. I was very impressed and scared.'

Vince smiled. 'It had its good side, too, right up until recent times. According to Francis, the stone had magical powers of life-giving and resurrection. The islanders carried their sick and dying folks here and held vigil.'

Faro shivered. 'What a splendid test. If exposure to the elements didn't kill them off then they would have survived anyway.'

'You're very cynical, Stepfather.'

Faro shook his head and said drily, 'I was merely thinking, how unfortunate that Francis did not try it on his wife.'

Vince gave him a hard look and said reproachfully, 'Francis has strong feelings for this place and its history. He would like to remove the Dwarfie Ha' stone by stone and have it taken to a safer site inland. But that would cost a lot of money. He had the same sort of idea about the family vault.' He sighed. 'Thora's will be the penultimate burial. When he dies, he has left orders for it to be sealed up for good.'

A sixteenth-century sarcophagus emblazoned with all the paraphernalia of death, skull and crossbones, weeping angels and hourglasses, had been almost obliterated by time and weather. Below, the Balfray vault was entered by a few steps leading down to an ancient iron-studded door.

Vince pointed to the sea-bitten wall behind them. Only the arched window indicated the remains of a religious house. 'Hard to picture it now but at one time the Balfray tomb was in the nave of the abbey. Its policies were bounded by a wall which stretched for some considerable distance towards the cliffs. Now only these few stones remain.'

Faro remembered the taciturn boatman's grisly tales about dead bodies as Vince continued, 'Worse than that, skeleton bones are sometimes found on the rocks below. There are apocryphal tales of skulls wearing diadems or hands still wearing rings worth a queen's ransom.'

Observing his stepfather's look of disbelief, he said, 'It's true enough to bring treasure-seekers rowing across from other islands. Word gets around. All it needs is for one fisherman to find a semi-valuable ring or brooch and flourish it in the local tavern at Kirkwall. In no time at all you'll have a fleet of the curious setting sail.'

Faro could see the reason in that. 'Quite understandable, since one small diamond or pearl would be worth more than a whole season's fishing.'

Vince nodded. 'And much less effort, much less danger to life and limb involved.'

'I shall bear it in mind. Perhaps some of these rock pools might be fished to advantage before we leave.'

'But don't you ever be tempted to go out on your own, Stepfather, unless you know about the tides. The sea comes in at the very devil of a lick, no gentle lapping the shore by way of warning, just one wild demoniac rush. So be warned. That was how Mrs Bliss was drowned.'

'Mrs Bliss?

'Yes, the last housekeeper at Balfray. The one Grandma replaced. It was all a tragic and quite unnecessary accident. Went out to rescue her little dog who got into difficulties and was cut off by the tide.'

'How very unfortunate. I thought all dogs could swim.'

'Not this one. No bigger than a squirrel and terrified of its own shadow. Apparently it had wandered out at low tide chasing something and once the sea came rushing in it was too scared to do anything but leap on a rock and bark.'

'And the housekeeper heard it?'

'Why yes, she was out searching the shore for the poor beast.' Vince shook his head. 'As I said, all tragic and unnecessary. Seems she hadn't been at Balfray long enough to take seriously the treacherous floodtide.'

'She was alone?'

'I imagine so.'

'Remarkable,' said Faro, and Vince looked at him sharply.

'It was an accident, I assure you.'

Faro nodded absently. A moment later he asked, 'Had she any family?'

'Not that I've heard of. From the Highlands somewhere. She's buried in the kirkyard. Grandma knows all about it. She'll fill you in on all the details. What's wrong?'

Faro had seized his arm. 'Take care. Someone's there . . . by the vault. Listen . . . '

Chapter Three

They were not in any danger.

As they listened, the sound became audible as stifled sobs from the far side of the Balfray sarcophagus.

A man crouched, arms cradling his knees, his head against the stone and, oblivious of their presence, he wept in abject misery.

Suddenly conscious of their shadows, he sprang to his feet and with one startled glance leaped away through the tombstones.

A bizarre eldritch figure, Faro caught one glimpse of a dead white face, huge haunted eyes and tangled hair streaming in the wind.

'Who on earth was that?' he asked, with a startled glance in Vince's direction. 'Not the bereaved husband, I hope.'

'No. That was Troller Jack, the blacksmith's brother. Not quite right in the head, alas. Thora Balfray was very good to him, patient and kind. She never dismissed him, as most folk did, as a simpleton to be mocked.

'Francis told me once that to her Troller was victim of some horrible disorder of the brain he could not control. She spent hours with him, even managed to teach him his letters. And, I gather, he worshipped her. He must have been here since the funeral, paying his own last respects. We must have given him a terrible fright.'

'No more than he gave us,' said Faro. 'He was like

some demon rising from the tomb. I'm glad you were with me.'

Vince laughed. 'Good heavens, Stepfather. Troller wouldn't harm a fly. You'll get used to his strange appearance.'

' "Selkie born and selkie reared," ' said Faro.

Vince asked him to repeat it.

'I don't know where it came from, lad. Something from my childhood, games we used to play. Nasty things we used to shout after folk who were daft. That they were seal people.'

'I'm glad you outgrew that, Stepfather. Sounds like Grandma's nonsense. Not quite in keeping with a detective inspector of police. What would Superintendent McIntosh say?' he added mockingly.

The grey skies erupted into a sudden fine drizzle and Faro was aware of being chilled to the bone. Disenchanted by his introduction to Balfray, he longed for a warm fire and a good dram inside him.

As they hurried in the direction of the drive, he asked, 'What was this about her being ill-wished, some nonsense like that? Did Francis ever explain?'

Vince hesitated for a moment. 'You're not going to like this, Stepfather.'

'Try me,' said Faro impatiently.

'When you asked me about the Balfray household and retainers, I didn't mention someone who is almost a member of the family, by habit and repute, constantly at Thora's side, her dear friend and companion.' He hesitated.

'Go on.'

'This friend is also reputed to be a witch. Most of the island gives her a wide berth.'

'Sensible, I suppose. But who the devil is she?'

Again Vince hesitated. 'As I said, Stepfather, you won't like this. I'm sorry, but it's Inga St Ola – our cousin Inga.'

Faro felt as if the breath had been knocked out of his body. His father Magnus and Inga's father had been remote cousins, boon companions and close as brothers. Like many other islanders who could trace their families back a few generations, they shared the same great-grandfather.

Inga and Jeremy had been childhood friends. There was a time while he was deciding whether to go to Edinburgh and join the police force when Faro considered asking her to be his wife.

Two years his senior, Inga had been his first love. She had adored him, and had given him – a secret known only to themselves – his initiation into the mysterious world of sex. After that he felt honour-bound, knowing he was leaving Orkney, to suggest marriage.

Her rejection of his stammered proposal hurt his pride but also brought an enormous sense of relief. Her reason? Yes, she did love him and there was no other man she would ever wish to marry but sadly she shook her head. He had one rival. The island. She loved it better than any man and could never ever leave Orkney. She would die, she told him solemnly, if she ever tried to cut that invisible tie which bound her to this land.

Faro's memory presented a vivid picture which had remained with him through the years of her rapt countenance as she said the words. He remembered too that loving her, while it made him feel so proud, so big and strong and manly possessing that fragile delicate body, he was afraid of her spirit.

Afraid of her dark powers, for even in those days she was already a selkie, a self-styled white witch, dabbling in all kinds of herbal mysteries and what she smilingly called her magic spells.

Her boast was that she could whistle up a wind, which was a profit if a sailor should find his bonny boat in the doldrums. But such abilities, as well as an undeniable talent for foretelling the future, only widened the gulf between herself and Jeremy Faro.

Such psychic gifts as second sight made him uncomfortable, at a loss for appropriate words. And they were too unnerving for the practical policeman in the making, who wished to cut himself adrift from his superstitious island upbringing.

In the early days, lonely in Edinburgh, he missed her, but he also realised that if word had got around that Constable Faro had a practising white witch as wife, this would have been a considerable handicap to his advancement.

Later he learned that after his departure from Orkney, Inga seemed to change her mind about leaving the island. His mother and the neighbours presumed that she had followed the handsome young policeman. Shaking their heads, they smiled indulgently. The next news would be of a wedding in Edinburgh, mark their words.

But Inga returned alone at Lammastide with the seals barking on the shore as if in a delirious chorus of welcome. Where had she been all that spring and summer, demanded the curious? But smiling, so happy to be home, she evaded all their questions, merely shaking her head as if bewildered, puzzled to know what all the fuss was about. Until at last they began to feel foolish, for it was as if she had been away on an errand to the mainland and absent for only a day and a night.

Faro was aware of Vince's hand on his arm. 'Look, Stepfather.'

Faro blinked against the rain. A girl was hurrying down the drive to meet them, shouting a greeting. His heart thudded in recognition, for it was as if his thoughts had uncannily conjured up Inga St Ola exactly as he had last seen her. Miraculously unchanged from his youth, tall, slim, she now stood before him.

He felt a sudden sickness, a feeling of doom at the pit of his stomach.

'Jeremy? Jeremy Faro, I thought it was yourself. The years have been good to you.' She laughed, pushing back long black hair unstreaked with grey. It was a gesture he remembered. Staring at him, hands on hips, her mouth and eyes wide open as if this was a huge joke, he noticed that her teeth, small and even, were still excellent.

She held out her hands. Here was a difference. These were not a young girl's hands, silken and thin-boned. These hands were no strangers to hard work, aged with toil, heavily veined, rough and calloused, freckled with what his mother called 'the flowers of death'.

But, apart from those work-worn hands, time had passed her by. While he stammered heaven only knew what platitudes and took in every detail of Inga St Ola, Faro was acutely aware of Vince's silent, somehow accusing presence at his elbow.

Inga was forty-two years old. Unlike the normal island wives who became shawled old women in their thirties, sea-wrinkled, bent with continual child-bearing and a bitter struggle against the elements, Inga with her long black hair unbound seemed little more than a girl.

Later Vince told him, 'Her youthful appearance goes against her too. All it does is add to her strange and sinister reputation. Envy, malice, the women hate her for it, especially those of her own age who have worn less well: this island woman has no right to be still beautiful past forty – unless she has sold her immortal soul to the Dark One.'

Added to physical beauty, Faro was aware of a swift-moving animal grace, still unfettered by time's passing. Did she still swim naked in the sea, he wondered, laughing at those who talked of seal people? He was curious, wanting to know what her life had been. Had she ever married? If not, then had she known many lovers?

While they mouthed trivialities at one another, his mind was burning with questions unasked. He was suddenly aware that the rain had steadily increased and with it Vince's hand impatient on his arm, urging him towards the front door.

Another delighted smile. Their ways parted with a promise to meet again and a bewildered Faro followed his stepson into the hall.

From the shadows Mary Faro emerged, drying her hands on her apron, and clasped her only son to her heart, rapturous at his unexpected appearance.

'Oh, son, I can hardly believe it's you. You never told me,' she reproached Vince.

'He wanted to surprise you.'

'And you did that, all right.' And linking arms with both of them she said, 'Well, I'm glad. I'm glad. Even if it is a melancholy time for you to come to this house.' And, standing on tiptoe, she kissed him again. 'You can have a room of your own, next to Vince. It's all very grand – not what we were used to in Kirkwall when you were a lad,' she continued as Faro was complimentary about a fine wide oak staircase leading up to a portrait gallery festooned with stags' heads, rising in a forest of antlers.

His mother proudly ushered him into an elegant and fashionable bedroom furnished in mahogany. Satisfied with his suitable exclamations of delight, she departed, carrying away wet garments and promising her two precious dears a nice pot of Earl Grey tea.

Faro sat down on the bed, slowly removed his boots. Staring at his feet, he was still hearing Inga's voice, her laugh, unable to obliterate her still-violent assault on his senses, that strong capable hand he had held. And Jeremy Faro, who prided himself on his total recall, the superb memory and observation which had helped him solve many a baffling crime, now made the disquieting deduction that he was unable to remember a single word of his conversation with Inga St Ola less than half an hour ago.

Awareness extended to Vince, silently staring out of the window, Faro realised how little the lad had contributed to the conversation with Inga. Quite unlike himself, since any attractive woman was a challenge. But this time gallantry, chivalry even, had been strangely absent.

Vince turned, aware of being the subject of that careful scrutiny. And, familiar over the years with his stepson's reactions, Faro knew that Inga's magic left that normally susceptible young man unmoved. In fact, without a word being spoken between them, he knew that his stepson heartily disliked her.

Mary Faro's imminent ascent of the stairs with the tea tray was announced by a twitter of tea cups. Faro sprang to his feet and shouted over the banisters, 'I'll have it down there, Mother, if it's convenient.'

'I'll come down later,' said Vince, leaning over his shoulder. 'Must change my boots. I'm afraid one of them is letting in water. Deuced uncomfortable,' he added, cutting short a reproachful homily from his stepgrandmother on the fatalities appertaining to wet feet.

Patting the box containing the Marsh Test apparatus, Vince nodded to Faro and, putting a finger to his lips, disappeared into his bedroom.

Mary Faro ushered Jeremy into the drawing-room. He exclaimed over magnificent proportions, handsome furniture, elegant mirrors and, dominating the room, two great bay windows which looked down over lawns to the south and west.

Here was a room that begged the visitor to enjoy peace and tranquillity. Not only providing an opportunity to enjoy a whole day's warmth and sunshine when the capricious weather allowed, the windows also offered an uninterrupted view of the sea with its pattern of islands.

Watching his mother set down the tea tray, he felt suddenly awed by his surroundings. He was, after all, merely the housekeeper's son. 'Are you sure? The kitchen would do excellently.'

'Not at all, dear. You're to be a guest here. Dr Balfray says so.'

'I must pay my condolences.'

'You'll have plenty of time later, dear. The poor love is in his study. He's hardly ever left it, apart from attending the funeral. Terrible, terrible this is for him. I just don't know how he is going to get through this evening. All these tenants coming for the wake – and their bequests.'

'Bequests?'

'Yes, dear. It's the rule of the Balfrays, established by the right- and proper-minded grandfather. When the laird or his lady dies, every tenant who comes to the wake is entitled to receive one golden guinea.'

'A very generous gesture, very commendable.'

Mary Faro nodded. 'They're a grand family. The best there is. But tell me about you, lad. What brought you here?'

Briefly touching on his last case which had left him standing on a quayside in the north of Scotland, Faro asked eagerly, 'Rose and Emily? How are they? Vince tells me they come over at the weekends.'

'Indeed they do, dear. I'd have liked fine to keep them here with me but Aunty said she would take them when the new term started . . .'

When he frowned, she added reproachfully, 'You surely haven't forgotten Aunty Griz who was so kind to you when you were a peedie bairn, after we lost your poor dear father . . . ?'

'Of course, of course,' lied Faro. 'Aunty Griz.'

'And she's so reliable. She loves them and they dote on her. I thought my place was with Mrs Balfray and

Dr Francis, when they were relying on me and now that he's alone I can't leave the poor doctor in the lurch,' she added, her eyes welling with tears.

'You did the right thing, Mother,' said Faro, patting her hand. 'A sad time for all of you. Vince tells me Mrs Balfray was greatly loved and that a lot of people helped to take care of her.'

Mrs Faro sniffed. 'Hardly a great lot.' And, enumerating on her fingers, she continued, 'Beside myself there was Miss Balfray, who is just heart-broken too. Reverend Erlandson, our nice minister she's engaged to, is a great comfort to her and to us all. And, of course, our Inga, as always the first to offer help to anyone.'

'I met her on the way in.'

'You did?' Mary Faro looked pleased. 'Well, well. She's such a sweet girl. So sad that she's never married. She'd have made a marvellous wife for someone.'

Again in that quick sideways glance he thought he detected a hint of reproach. Did his mother still think that someone should have been himself?

'The years have been very good to her, I thought.'

'Indeed they have.' Mrs Faro beamed. 'She's a lovely girl, always was, and it goes all the way through, despite the nastiness of some folk here.'

'How's that, Mother?'

'Oh you know, Jeremy. Even when you were a lad there was all this talk about her being a selkie. And her doing nothing but good. Always ready with her herbs and the like and I've seen her with my own eyes breathe life into a dying bairn. But some folk can never be satisfied. Just be a peedie bit different . . .'

She shrugged, pausing to refill his cup. 'There were rumours that she'd brought other sick people back to life. And you know what folk said? What kind of life was that if it cost them their immortal souls. They thought that was what she did, stole their souls for the devil.'

'What brought her to Balfray?'

'She came years back. When Saul Hoy's mother died. Saul's the smithy and they were distantly related to your poor dear father by marriage. Anyway, Saul was left with this simple brother, they call him Troller Jack, and Inga came to look after him when he was ill. The laddie just doted on her, she could do anything with him and she just stayed on.'

She gave him a hesitant look. 'There was talk about her marrying Saul. But it never came to anything. There's plenty that snigger about that, too, and would like to say that she's a bad woman.'

Faro smiled. His mother would have been the first to make comments on anyone but Inga living in the same house as a bachelor, both of them of marriageable years. 'You know how island folk gossip. What can you expect them to say?'

'I would say that's her own business,' snorted Mary Faro. 'But I'll tell you because she's kin. She told me once that she might have married him but she learned from her mother before she died that he was her half-brother. Isn't that awful?'

Faro smiled. It was not an unknown occurrence.

'Wasn't that a terrible thing to find out?' asked Mary Faro in shocked tones.

'Better found out before than after marriage.'

Mrs Faro hesitated a moment then went on. 'If there have been any sweethearts in her life, past or present, then this is Inga's biggest secret of all. Luckily her reputation keeps the men hereabouts at bay. You can see them eyeing her, especially when it's harvest time and they've had a few drams, but none of them would harm her. In fact, they're too scared to lay a hand on her.' Mary Faro chuckled. 'They know all about what crossing a witch can do to a man, their wives have made sure of that.'

And suddenly confidential, she leaned forward and touched his arm. 'You know what I think? I think she's still sweet on you. You were her one and only.'

'Childhood sweethearts, Mother. Few of them ever walk down the aisle together.'

'You needn't laugh. Maybe it's like that in Edinburgh with all those temptations, all those wicked ways,' she said crossly, 'but here in Orkney people are different. Couples meet when they're bairns, often still at the school, and grow up to get married. They love only once, like your poor dear father and me— '

She was interrupted by the sound of footsteps outside the door.

The newcomer was Dr Francis Balfray. His ashen countenance, his unshaven unkempt appearance, told a poignant tale of sorrow before which Faro's condolences were lost.

Indeed, Faro doubted whether he heard them at all, they seemed such a totally inadequate drop in that ocean of despair.

Had he eaten today? Would he like a nice cup of tea?

Faro listened in amazement to his mother's bright stab at normality, her brave smiles in Balfray's direction. She was doing her best, bless her heart, but what was food and drink to a man at such a time as this?

Vince arrived and Faro observed the obvious sympathy between the two young men which relieved the awkward situation. His stepson seemed to have hit the exact chord of what was right in these doleful circumstances.

Watching them, he was glad to see that their postgraduate meeting had turned a polite acquaintance into what looked like the beginnings of close friendship. If tact and compromise were at work, then Vince would make a splendid general practitioner in medicine.

'I heard voices and thought I might find Captain Gibb

and Norma. Arrangements, you know . . . for . . . for this evening.'

Mary Faro said she hadn't seen them, but that the Captain was probably in the library with his books.

Francis nodded absently and at the door again remembered the courtesy due to the unexpected guest.

His smile was forced, his hand unsteady. 'Do make yourself at home, Mr Faro. You are most welcome to Balfray.' And, having fulfilled the ancient obligations of a laird to the stranger under his roof, he gratefully took his departure.

Vince drank his tea, ate his buttered scones with an alarming speed that would have crippled Faro with a digestive upset for several days. All the while he managed to include an affectionate repartee with his stepgrandmother who so obviously adored him. Then, declining further refreshment, he made his exit, his slight gesture indicating that Faro should follow him.

Once in the bedroom, Faro said, 'Well?'

'Not well at all, Stepfather. The test in both cases is positive. Come and look at this.'

Faro inspected the simple apparatus set up on the desk. The ingenuous but amazingly sensitive device which recovered the arsenic was a metallic mirror on a piece of porcelain.

Looking over his shoulder, Vince said, 'There are 3.20 grains of arsenic present.'

Faro whistled. 'And two grains is a fatal dose, is it not?'

'Correct. And we have enough here in both samples to cause Thora Balfray's death. She was murdered, Stepfather. There is no longer the least doubt about that.'

Chapter Four

Faro sat down on the bed. 'So you were right. I was hoping you'd be wrong, you know.'

'So was I.'

'There's no doubt whatsoever?'

'None at all. Thora Balfray was poisoned.'

'Where do we go from here?'

'Suppose you tell me. You're the policeman.'

Faro looked at him sharply.

'I'm sorry, Stepfather, but at this moment I wish to God I'd never heard of the Marsh Test and that after I'd signed the death certificate I'd been able to persuade my conscience that Thora died of natural causes.'

Beating his fists upon the bedpost in a furious gesture, he swung round to face his stepfather. 'Why the hell didn't I leave well alone? Answer me that if you can.'

'Because it wasn't well, lad. Because someone murdered Thora Balfray and, if you hadn't done something about it, your conscience would have plagued you for the rest of your life. Besides, you owe it to Francis.'

Vince laughed bitterly. 'Oh yes, and he is going to love me for that. His suffering has only just begun. Losing Thora was merely the beginning of the nightmare of what he will now have to endure.'

'Listen,' said Faro sternly. 'I know exactly how you feel. Many's the time I've suspected, aye, known, that murder has been committed, and I've been so sorry for the innocent folks involved that I've been tempted, even wished, as you are wishing, that I'd never poked and probed into the whole sorry business.'

Vince had taken to pacing the floor angrily, as if to thrust out the force of his stepfather's words.

'Your first debt, lad, let me remind you, is not to Francis Balfray. It is to his wife, an unfortunate young woman, loved by all for her many virtues it seems, who was put to an agonising slow death by someone close to her. Someone I don't doubt that she loved and trusted. You know as well as I do that arsenic has always been the most popular and easiest way of getting rid of unwanted relatives. It began with the Caesars, so much in demand in Imperial Rome that food tasters were as numerous and as necessary as chefs.'

'Very popular with the Borgias, too, I seem to remember, Stepfather. "Le poudre de succession", that's what the French call it.'

'And with good reason. You're being blinded by the closeness of these tragic events around you, Vince. But I beg you, cast all sentiment aside and think calmly and coldly about what really happened and why.'

Vince gave him a horrified look. 'You mean that until we know the motive for Thora's death, some other member of the family might also be in danger. Is that it?'

Leaning on the table, Faro continued, 'Precisely. We now have a murderer on the loose and having got away with it once, he – or she – might decide to strike again. I'm presuming that Francis stood to gain by his wife's death and so he must be watched very carefully.'

Vince sat down suddenly. 'Come to think of it, he told me something, oh, just last week. He was riding back from the harbour along the cliff path after dark when someone leaped out waving a cloak or something. His horse was terrified and threw him, luckily on to the grassy slope. But they both had a lucky escape – another yard and they would have been over the cliff and into the sea. Very nearly a tragedy. Doesn't bear thinking about,' he added with a shudder and, springing to his feet, he looked down at his stepfather. 'Poor old Francis, I wish you could have seen him. He staggered in, all muddied and shaken. Got the fright of his life, although he passed it off as a practical joke.'

'Some joke,' said Faro grimly.

Vince looked at the mantelpiece clock. 'We'd better start dressing for dinner. Too late to summon the Procurator Fiscal, I suppose, even presuming we could get a boat to take us to Kirkwall.'

'I doubt that would be a popular request with everyone preparing for the wake. Besides, he'd hardly welcome being summoned at this hour.'

Vince's sigh sounded suspiciously relieved. 'If I'm for the chop I'm glad to delay the evil hour.'

'Let's not think about that, lad. There were extenuating circumstances. After all, you're a young doctor . . .'

'Please don't make excuses for me, Stepfather. I'm making enough for myself without your help. And whatever you say by consolation doesn't alter the fact that I compounded a felony. I'd like to get it over as soon as I can, so can we now talk about motives and opportunities?

'She was an heiress in her own right, distaff side. Francis inherits her fortune and, as there is no direct heir in the event of his demise, Thora willed everything to Norma Balfray. Thora was the child of Sir Joseph's second marriage, so she could only inherit Balfray if she outlived her stepsister.'

'Interesting,' said Faro thoughtfully.

'Norma inherited a penniless Balfray, heavily in debt. As for Francis, he has no direct claim to it. He belongs to a cadet branch of the family – you can look at the family tree sometime if you're interested. They share the same great-great-grandfather.'

'Sounds like everyone else in Orkney, when you go back that far.'

Vince smiled. 'Francis has been a constant visitor since his childhood. Sir Joseph was very fond of him – the son he never had. When he put Francis through medical school it was implicitly understood that he set up practice as resident doctor in the castle, for the benefit of his tenants, and be referred to by the courtesy title of "laird". Sir Joseph had another reason. Francis and Norma had been childhood sweethearts and he approved of the match.

'Sadly, it didn't work out like that at all and Francis married Thora instead, who insisted that Norma be made a generous allowance.'

Faro gave him a cynical smile. 'Decent of her, in the circumstances. And, although Thora might be termed the goose with the golden eggs where Norma was concerned, let us not forget that fortunes are not the sole reason for murdering close kin.'

'No one in the household would have harmed her, that's for sure. They all made their devotion to her perfectly clear. Ask Grandma, she'll tell you. Nothing much passes her by in the way of gossip.'

Faro considered for a moment. 'What about opportunity? Administering poison without giving a dose massive enough for immediate demise means constant access, for just a little at a time.'

Vince laughed grimly. 'Opportunity certainly wasn't lacking. Grandma tells me that everyone in the household was trying to tempt her jaded appetite: egg nog, soup, tonics, home-made remedies,' he enumerated. 'And for those with less noble motives every country house and estate has access to arsenic in the form of rat poison.'

'Who chiefly nursed her?'

'Norma. She was with her almost constantly, except when she was relieved by Grandma— ' there was the slightest hesitation ' —or Inga.'

'You mentioned jealousy. There was no enmity between the stepsisters?'

Vince shook his head. 'None that was apparent. To any observer they seemed devoted to each other.'

'Despite the fact that Thora stole Francis? And that generous allowance might have been less charitably regarded by Norma as conscience money?'

'Oh, that was forgotten, and, I imagine, forgiven long ago. Especially as Norma found happiness elsewhere. She is going to marry Reverend Erlandson, the family priest.'

'Priest? I thought you said he was a minister.'

Vince laughed. 'Not of the Church of Scotland. The Balfrays are Episcopalians. In my opinion, the services are just one step removed from Roman Catholicism. Probably the Balfrays compromised on religion,' he added doubtfully. 'They've remained staunch Jacobites in our stronghold of Calvinism.'

Faro smiled. 'My first thought when I arrived in Balfray was that if Bonnie Prince Charlie had returned to Scotland in 1845 and had included Orkney in his triumphal itinerary, he wouldn't have noticed a great deal of difference in the passing of over a hundred years.'

He paused and added, 'I shouldn't have imagined there was much call for a resident churchman in a place the size of Balfray.'

'There isn't. Erlandson has one or two other parishes that he serves. Mostly by boat if the weather and the tide are right.'

'Interesting.'

'He's very enlightened, you know. He and Norma are deeply enamoured of each other.' He smiled. 'You'll see. Much in love and don't care who knows it.'

Faro laughed. 'Indeed. Then I shall look forward to meeting our resident chaplain and his lady love. What about kitchen staff?'

'Norma is nominally in charge of housekeeper, maids and so forth. But even she retired gracefully when Grandma took over from the last housekeeper, the one who was drowned.'

'Oh yes, the unfortunate Mrs Bliss.' Faro placed his fingertips together and studied them thoughtfully. 'And so, Vince, what are your present theories about who might have wanted rid of Mrs Balfray?'

'Theories are easy, Stepfather.' Vince hesitated. 'I'd like you to meet the family and form some ideas of your own, then we'll talk about my theories.'

'Before that melancholy confrontation, it would help if you would bring me up to date on all that has happened since you arrived on the island.'

'There isn't much to tell.' Vince sighed. 'Do you really want me to go right back to the beginning?'

'If you would be so good.'

'It was obvious the moment I arrived here that I was too late, that Thora was on the point of death. There was nothing I, or anyone, could do to save her. She lingered in a coma for a day or two but I was too late to do anything but comfort her husband as she breathed her last.'

Vince stared gloomily into space. 'A terrible scene, Stepfather, one I shall never forget. Francis sobbing, calling her name, shouting that he couldn't believe it, wouldn't believe it. As if the whole tragic business had happened quite suddenly without any warning. You know the sort of thing I'm talking about. God knows you had it with Mama . . . '

Vince paused and gripped Faro's arm as if in apology for mentioning the subject still so painful to both of them. 'But this was different. She hadn't been taken ill and snatched from him. As a doctor, he must have known by her wasted body, by the steady decline, that she had not long to live.' With a sigh he added, 'Everyone else in the household, although they maintained attitudes of cheery hopefulness for Francis' sake, they all knew she was going to die.'

As he fell silent Faro said, 'Even when we expect death, lad, we always keep hoping for a miracle that will divert it from our own door – that the man with the scythe will decide to pass us by.'

Vince shivered. 'She was, by all accounts, a very remarkable lady. A great pity you'll never have a chance to meet her now.'

In that Vince was wrong. Faro was to see Thora Balfray very soon and in the most unexpected of macabre circumstances.

The nausea that had been threatening ever since he arrived on Balfray, a product of unwise eating on the ferry, seized Faro in a violent attack of sickness as he was about to set foot in the great hall where the laird's loyal tenants waited respectfully to receive from his hands their golden guineas.

Faro reached his room in time and afterwards lay sweating feverishly on his bed as the waves of griping pain swept over him. In the light of what was to come, he was infinitely to regret having missed Thora Balfray's wake. His absence was noted by Vince who came in search of him as soon as he could reasonably leave. He gazed at his stepfather's ashen countenance in some alarm and quickly mixed a sedative.

A few minutes later, Faro announced that he felt considerably better while Vince continued to chide him about his confounded eating habits, his careless lifestyle.

'Stop it, Vince. Stop it at once. It's bad enough having a miserable stomach upset without a lecture that would do my mother proud. And I'll strangle you, lad, if you breathe a word of this to her. Now, tell me about the wake.'

'All very feudal. I'm sorry you missed it. Almost a return to the Barony courts of old. Poor Francis, he's a fine solid laird, exactly what this island needs. Never spares himself where the welfare of the tenants is concerned. You'll see what he's done for agriculture, not to mention a drainage system and sanitation almost non-existent before Sir Joseph's day.'

As he listened, Faro found himself remembering that earlier conversation with his stepson in Edinburgh when Francis Balfray's letter had arrived. He remarked on the improvement in their relationship.

Vince smiled. 'Yes, I like him a lot and respect him. Seeing him through the traumas of this last week has added a new dimension to poor old Francis.' He shrugged. 'At medical school, we didn't have a lot in common. He wasn't exactly popular. Bit of a swot. Not good at athletics.'

'Perhaps he was just too poor to stand his round of drinks.'

'How did you guess that?'

'Students being put through college by relatives are frequently impoverished. And you have already volunteered that piece of information.'

Vince looked shamefaced. 'I think I guessed something of the sort at the time. He didn't strike me as being mean, but he had to be careful. Now I know why. Francis had no rich father's fortune to squander. He was an idealist and under a moral obligation to Sir Joseph. Observing him in company, standing back, I knew his pride suffered and in a way it made me kinder to him.'

He shrugged. 'I made plenty of excuses for him, but Rob and Walter disliked him intensely, didn't want him trailing around with us. He didn't womanise either, a little stuffy, terribly respectable. No Leith Walk howffs for Francis. There was this sweetheart in Orkney he mooned about, never tired of telling us how marvellous she was and how he was going back to marry his Miss Balfray.'

'Very admirable and loyal. And so they were married.'

'Well, yes . . . and no, Stepfather. He didn't marry her.'

'I thought . . . '

'I mean it was Thora he married, not Norma. Yet I could have sworn the elder sister was his intended.'

'Of course, if he referred to her as Miss Balfray, the younger sister would be known by her Christian name – Miss Thora Balfray.'

'When I arrived I nearly put my foot in it, I can tell you. I was quite taken aback to find that he'd married the wrong sister, especially as Thora was, well, not to put too fine a point on it, rather plain.'

Faro smiled. 'You put too much importance on looks, lad. They aren't, and never will be, everything a man needs in a wife. Perhaps on closer acquaintance Francis discovered that Thora had a nicer nature. How did Norma react to being jilted by her lover?'

'They all continued to live in the castle while Francis set up his medical practice. It was Norma's home after all. She had very little option to move elsewhere, being virtually penniless until Thora came forward with an allowance to save her pride. But her closeness to Thora who she nursed devotedly suggested that there was no jealousy between the stepsisters, especially when she became engaged to John Erlandson.'

'When did this happen?'

Vince thought. 'Fairly recently, soon after Erlandson came to Balfray. Love at first sight, I gather, and neither of them in the first flush of youth. Norma is older than Francis, you know. Anyway, she and John are a very sentimental pair, very romantic. None of this stiff upper lip in company as befits a man of the cloth and so forth.' He smiled. 'A pretty sight they make, but not everyone approves. Some of the older island folk feel that the chaplain is a little lacking in dignity and too easy-going in general.'

'That will make a pleasant change, don't you think?'

As bigotry was one of his stepfather's favourite hobby-horses, Vince said hastily, 'You must come to the Balfray chapel and hear him preach.'

'I'm not sure whether I'm quite ready for that.'

Vince laughed. 'Come now, Stepfather. Everyone goes to church here, it's the social event of the week, with Norma sitting in the front pew looking proud as Punch.'

'Did Francis ever explain the sudden change in betrothed?'

'No, he merely implied that I had got the wrong end of the stick.'

'As well you might. Thora, Norma. The names are sufficiently similar for anyone to make a mistake.'

Vince shook his head. 'It was definitely Miss Balfray – Norma. He told us how lovely she was. No one could ever have described Thora as pretty, let alone lovely.'

'Love is well known for its blindness, lad. She might have seemed so to a besotted lover.'

In the pause that followed, Faro was overwhelmed by a sudden yearning to know whether Inga was at the wake and if she had expressed any anxiety about his absence.

Instead he asked, 'Mother wasn't curious to know where I was this evening?'

'She didn't comment upon it.'

'Thank God for that.' The last thing he wanted was for his mother to know of his malaise and come pounding upstairs with trays of her special vile-tasting remedies accompanied by the firm pronouncement, 'They made you well when you were a peedie lad and they'll still work. Nothing like old-fashioned cures for an upset stomach.'

'She didn't seem to think your absence in any way odd.'

'What about Francis?'

'I don't imagine he even noticed it. He wouldn't expect you to attend the wake when you had just arrived on the island. He went through the whole evening gallantly, in a daze of grief. I imagine he won't remember a moment of it. And, after all, it wasn't as if you had known Thora.'

So saying, Vince stood up and stretched his arms above his head. 'Well, if you're sure you're feeling better, I think I shall retire. Call me if you need anything.'

'I think I'll live until morning. Before you go, would you open the window?'

Vince did as he was asked. There was a moon swaying unsteadily through racing clouds. The sound of barking rose, a weird lament from the shore.

'The seals are noisy tonight. The islanders will all be shaking their heads, those sober enough to dare, that is, and saying that they too are mourning the lady of Balfray.'

Faro shivered. 'I would have laughed at you in Edinburgh if you'd made such a statement. But here . . . ' He shrugged.

'I know, here anything seems possible, doesn't it? An extra sense that perhaps we were all born with, but living in cities we lost contact with the earth.'

Faro smiled. 'You're right, lad. We've successfully

buried our sixth sense under tons of bricks and mortar.'

Instead of leaving, Vince sat down on the edge of the bed and regarded him solemnly. 'There are dark gods here, darker than a Presbyterian Sunday in Newington, Stepfather. I can feel it, and I'm learning about you. Here you take on another dimension. Even in the short time you've been here, I hardly recognise you.'

'Come, lad, what nonsense.'

'Don't laugh at me, Stepfather. It's true. How could you ever belong to that other world we've left in Edinburgh, to Sheridan Place and Mrs Brook and afternoon tea on a silver tray?'

And even though they both laughed, Vince thought that looking at Faro was like watching the shedding of many generations. Here was the ultimate Viking, the man who had stepped back in time and was one with the wild seas, the bird-haunted mockery from cliff and sky.

He was amazed to find that his stepfather seemed to have grown in stature and he suspected that this Detective Inspector Faro was an infinitely more formidable opponent to the murderer of Thora Balfray than to the criminals in Edinburgh's High Street.

Suddenly, without quite knowing why, Vince was afraid.

Fear is catching and knowing that his astute stepson was right, Faro lay restlessly wide awake. Here his roots were deeply entrenched and he could never quite escape. His beginnings: superstitious, ignorant, and fraught with omens, with ancient gods to be placated, creatures to be revered and avoided.

Strange that, even as a man of forty, the senses of childhood were undiminished. Sounds and scents and textures lured back the laughing father he barely remembered in Edinburgh. Here in Orkney, most disturbing of all, a glimpse of Inga St Ola brought back vivid memories and set his mind fleeing down a path that led to the all-devouring ecstasies of first love.

At last he fell asleep, as his ancestors had done for more than a thousand years, to the elemental call from the seals on the rocks far below the house and the susurrus of the floodtide beating upon the shore.

It was a cry that awakened him. A human cry of terror.

Chapter Five

The cry was swiftly followed by a door banging. Another cry dispelled any notion that this might have been part of a dream. The sound of running footsteps had Faro wide awake and leaping out of bed. He was seizing a robe when the door opened and his mother rushed in.

'Oh, Jeremy, come quickly. But you can't go out like that, dear, you'll need your outdoor clothes. There's been a terrible accident. In the kirkyard . . . '

As he pulled on trousers and a shirt, she continued breathlessly, 'Mr Erlandson came and told us, he's gone back to see if he could do anything.'

'What happened, Mother? Who's been hurt?'

'I don't know. He just said what I've told you. There's been a terrible accident and I was to get Vince to come immediately. He didn't want Dr Francis to go back with him, so it must have been something dreadful. I heard them arguing. "I urge you to stay here, I implore you," ' she said dramatically. 'Those were his exact words—'

She was interrupted by Vince, fully dressed, looking round the door. A few minutes later the two men were hurrying down to the kirkyard, where torches blazing near the Balfray vault suggested that a small crowd had already gathered.

Pushing his way through, Faro beheld a macabre sight. The flickering light, a torch held high over the Odin Stone, revealed two figures lying side by side. One was Troller Jack, whose grief-stricken sojourn by

Thora Balfray's tomb he and Vince had interrupted on their cliff-top walk. And stretched out beside him was the corpse of a young woman.

The condition of her grave-clothes indicated that she had been newly interred and the fact that decomposition had not yet destroyed her features made Vince's horrified whisper quite unnecessary. At that moment an awakening breeze ruffled the satin and lace of the wedding dress she had been buried in, giving an uneasy illusion of life to the disinterred corpse of Thora Balfray.

Faro wondered if he was still dreaming. The setting, eerily lit by flickering torches and a moon scurrying between storm-tossed clouds, with seals barking and the elemental sea sounding on the cliffs below, seemed utterly detached from reality.

Again he blinked incredulously at this reconstruction of the death scene from the last act of *Romeo and Juliet*. There was only one difference: this macabre Juliet had been dead for several days. Horrifying as it was, the first consideration was Troller Jack. Vince was already bending over him.

'No need for that, sir. He's dead. I've already tried to revive him without success.' The speaker was a young man who smelt strongly of whisky.

'And who might you be?' demanded Faro.

'Sergeant Frith, Kirkwall Police.'

Faro smiled. 'Well done. You arrived here with amazing promptitude. Congratulations.'

Frith stared at him and then saluted smartly. 'You must be Inspector Faro. I was hoping to have a word with you.'

At Faro's astonished expression, he gave a somewhat sheepish grin. 'I was here already, sir. Came to the wake. The Friths have served the laird's family for three generations. My dad was factor until he died two years ago.' He nodded in the direction of the tall thin man who approached. 'Minister came for me when he found Troller.'

'Is he . . . is he . . . ?' enquired the minister.

Faro nodded. Even without the clerical collar, ascetic features, with their Imperial beard reminiscent of a saint from a medieval fresco, identified Reverend John Erlandson.

'I'm afraid so.'

'Dear God, how awful. I couldn't move him, but I hoped he was only injured. Dear God. To do such a thing.' The minister covered his face with his hands, overcome by grief.

Vince turned to Faro. 'It must have happened very recently. His body is still warm and' he added in a whisper 'still bleeding.' And pointing towards the other corpse, he said to Erlandson, 'Does Francis know?'

Erlandson nodded miserably. 'There was no way I could spare him. I tried to keep it from him, told him only about Troller but he insisted on coming to see for himself. It was dreadful, dreadful. As long as I live I shall never forget his face when he saw her lying there.'

'Where is he now?' Vince demanded.

'He is in a state of collapse, complete collapse. Captain Gibb has kindly taken care of him. I believe they went to the Tower, the house the Captain leases from Dr Balfray.' And, wringing his hands, he whispered, 'Dear God, what are we to do . . . ?'

But Faro was no longer listening. Closely observed by Sergeant Frith, whose balance was none too steady, he touched Troller's still bleeding hands, his clothes wringing wet. Beneath his head a trickle of blood ran down the stone, uncomfortably reminiscent of the sacrificial legend.

Faro frowned. The Odin Stone itself was quite dry. Why should it be wet all around Troller yet just a foot away Thora Balfray's grave-clothes were bone dry? He walked round the stone examining the grass, Frith at his heels. 'Has anyone but yourself walked round here?'

Frith gave a bewildered shake of his head. 'Maybe. I don't think so. Reverend Erlandson and I were the first ones here . . . '

Faro pointed to the watchers who gathered a few yards away, their silent ranks broken only by an occasional murmur, a woman's sob. 'Are you sure?' he asked.

'Look at them, sir. See how afraid they are. It did not take much persuasion from me, I can tell you, to keep them at a distance.'

'I implored them to go home immediately, I wanted to spare my little flock this dreadful scene,' added the minister agitatedly as he again turned to the scene on the Odin Stone. 'I cannot imagine Troller doing such a wicked act as this.'

He looked across at the crowd which had grown, with torches approaching singly or in bands from the village. He made a helpless gesture. 'What devil put such an idea as this into his poor sick mind?'

'I'm not sure what you mean, sir,' Faro interrupted.

Erlandson frowned grimly. 'The resurrection stone, that's what the heathens of old called it. That it could heal the sick and bring dead lovers back to life.'

He paused to let the words sink in and continued. 'Preposterous, I know that's what you're thinking, gentlemen. Superstitious nonsense, but in spite of our teachings these ideas die hard. But to do this, to hint that poor Mrs Balfray could be brought back to life.'

He shook his head angrily. 'It's quite intolerable and I still cannot believe the evidence of my own eyes. Simple, Troller Jack was, and immensely strong, but quite, quite harmless. He loved animals and children and they trusted him.'

'We encountered him this afternoon, sir,' said Vince.

'He was crouched by the vault here, sobbing his heart out, poor chap.'

'Is that so?' asked the minister. 'He was utterly distraught when Mrs Balfray died, so perhaps we should have been prepared for something like this. If only I had known, been able to offer him words of comfort from the Gospels. I blame myself, Dr Laurie, I should have guessed . . . '

'No one could guess the reactions of a sick child-like mind,' said Vince. 'Thora's death must have been his final break with reality. It isn't all that unusual. Grief can destroy even quite normal folk, you know.'

'Is that so? Then it is now poor Dr Balfray we must watch. Yes, we must be vigilant.' Erlandson, bewildered, nodded vigorously, his gaze returned again to the scene on the Odin Stone. 'But to take her from her last resting place,' he repeated. 'Troller had a good Christian upbringing, gentlemen, came to church each Sunday.'

As he spoke a woman emerged from the crowd and, with a brief curtsy, produced a rough blanket. The minister covered Thora's corpse, for the wind had taken on a boisterous turn and was tugging at the elaborate shroud, billowing it out from her emaciated body into a macabre imitation of life.

Faro heard slurred voices from the little crowd. 'Is it a joke then?' 'Hush, Geordie.'

He stared thoughtfully over Vince's shoulder as he returned to his examination of the dead man, studying the watchers closely for the first time. Torches were being doused, they were no longer necessary. And in that pale but sharp and clear dawn light on the cliff top, he saw the genuinely shocked, the shocked but curious and in many cases the far from sober countenances, swaying unsteadily, hiccuping with vacant grins of disbelief.

A sound to his left indicated that Sergeant Frith had

retreated behind a tombstone to be violently sick. Faro sighed deeply.

'Let me through, let me through.'

The newcomer was Francis Balfray. He stared at the blanket-covered figure and dragged himself forward as, swaying, he clutched at Captain Gibb who tried to support him.

'Francis, Francis, come away. There's nothing you can do.' And addressing Faro, Gibb said, 'I couldn't keep him away . . . '

Francis leaned forward heavily, his hands on the Odin Stone. 'Oh no, I shan't come away, not yet, not yet. This is my wife . . . my wife who's lying here. And I shan't rest until I find out who did this . . . this horror . . . '

Three head-shawled women came forward to comfort him. They were like the furies in a play, thought Faro, recognising his mother and Inga St Ola supporting a weeping woman who could only be Norma Balfray.

The minister gathered them into his arms. Only he who had had the worst shock of all, the discovery of the two bodies, now seemed able to deal with the situation.

Faro was suddenly painfully aware of Inga's expressionless face, strangely detached from this scene of horror with eyes only for the man who had come back into her own life after twenty years.

After that first glance, Faro assiduously avoided looking in her direction. Devoting his attention to the Odin Stone he decided that whoever had stage-managed this scene had a keen sense of theatre. It was in the best traditions of a Wagnerian opera.

'Easy to see what happened. Young lad hopelessly enamoured of a married lady beyond his station in life,' said Sergeant Frith, who had returned to the fray and was looking considerably relieved. 'Lady died of a wasting disease and he tried to bring her back to life, remembering the powers of the Odin Stone. When that doesn't work, he does himself in.'

Faro regarded him heavily, wondering what on earth Frith read in his off-duty hours.

'I'll let the Fiscal know. He'll need to have a look. But there's no need for concern. Suicide while of an unsound mind. Happens all the time. Open and shut case, gentlemen,' Frith added firmly, buttoning up his coat as if he regretted the absence of his policeman's uniform.

Faro sighed again. This plot sounded much too clever for a simple-minded village lad to dream up, especially as Troller's association with the dead woman, he was to learn later, had been perfectly innocent. He had visited the castle almost every day to bring her a bunch of wild flowers. As for Francis, he had cast a kind and compassionate eye on the lad's infatuation.

Faro looked at Francis. The two deaths, even to those uninvolved, were cause for indignation and distress, but how much worse for the bereaved husband to find his dead wife laid out beside the village simpleton on the ancient stone of sacrifice. Two bodies, side by side, one still warm, one a week-old corpse, was against all the bounds of decency. Who could have played such a monstrous trick?

As the three women and Captain Gibb almost bodily removed the fainting laird from the scene, Sergeant Frith took the opportunity of being in command to address the crowd. 'Return to your homes, all of you, please. Nothing more to see.' He beckoned Erlandson aside. 'The corpse had better go back into the crypt. Regarding the deceased, I see no reason why he shouldn't be taken to his home—'

'One moment, please.' Vince stepped forward. 'I am assistant to the police surgeon with Edinburgh City Police and I should like to conduct a thorough examination of the body.'

'As you please,' said Frith, his weary tone indicating that it was a mere waste of time. 'I'm away to see if I can get across to Kirkwall. May I leave you in charge, Inspector?' And as the crowd were slow to disperse, he said to Erlandson, 'Would you – please?'

Stirring from his reverie, Erlandson said, 'Of course, of course.' And, holding up his arms wide in a gesture of benediction, he addressed the islanders. 'There is nothing any of you can do. Please return to your homes and God go with you.'

The watchers, who had increased with the growing daylight, now dispersed at his command, but with considerable reluctance and many backward glances. Their curiosity and appetite for the sensational was one Faro frequently encountered at a hanging in Edinburgh.

But for Balfray this was a new experience. Nothing as sensational as the scene they were witnessing on the Odin Stone had ever happened in their lives before. One day it, too, would go down in legend.

Watching Sergeant Frith depart, Erlandson indicated Thora's corpse. 'The coffin must be about somewhere.'

They followed him into the vault where Faro relieved him of the torch for a closer look. They were in a tiny stone room and one glance was sufficient to convince Faro that the Balfray family vault had been adapted from a prehistoric chambered tomb.

He knew from such burial chambers that the main purpose of the stone shelves in the walls had been to hold the dead in a series of rectangular chambers subdivided by pairs of upright slabs into individual ledges or burial lairs. The foremost example was Maes Howe, excavated only ten years earlier, in 1861, when he and Lizzie were spending their honeymoon in Orkney.

By the flickering torchlight, the Balfray vault was revealed as only one part of what had once been perhaps a huge chambered cairn, entered by a long low stone passage. Considering its nearness to the cliff edge, it was not difficult to imagine what had become of most of the original structure, reclaimed by the sea.

A decidedly unpleasant atmosphere of decay and corruption lingered about several mouldering coffins, indicating the last resting places of bygone Balfrays. Taking command of the torch, Faro continued his minute search of the vault, examining ledges, floor and walls for some clue to Thora Balfray's remarkable resurrection.

The vault was small and, with each passing moment, less inviting. Space to move freely was severely limited and he had to ask Erlandson and Vince to step aside. The minister regarded these requests in the manner of one humouring a madman, adding a grunt of disapproval as Faro knelt by the open and now empty coffin on the floor of the vault.

The walls of the vault were innocent of any inscription which might identify their place in history, let alone incriminate a murderer, but Faro raised the torch for a final inspection. Above the ledge which Thora Balfray's coffin had occupied was the carving of a large insect, a bee.

'Part of the family crest?' he asked Erlandson.

'I have no idea.' The minister peered over his shoulder. 'A bee. How interesting. I've never noticed it before. I'm told that this was once the crypt of the original castle,' he whispered. 'But it goes back a great deal further in time.'

Faro looked round. 'It does indeed.'

Erlandson seemed ill at ease. He looked longingly towards the entrance. 'Exactly so. Exactly so. Probably the same date as the Dwarfie Ha'.' He indicated the empty coffin. 'If you two gentlemen would be so good as to assist me . . . '

Contact at close quarters with the cold clammy body,

already wreathed in the unpleasant stench of corruption, brought a further dimension of nightmare to their activities. This was definitely not for the squeamish, thought Faro, only the strongest of stomachs would not have rebelled.

However, considering the nature of Erlandson's mission in life and death and Vince's encounters with corpses as an everyday occurrence, the three men succeeded very well in restoring the late Thora Balfray to her coffin once more.

As they prepared to leave the vault, Faro said to Erlandson, 'Be good enough to leave the door unlocked, sir. I need to make sure of certain facts . . . evidence,' he ended lamely.

'Feel free to do so, for there is no lock. The door is sealed by the laird after each interment. As for your evidence,' he added wearily, 'there can be nothing in there that is not immediately visible. All that happened in the crypt is that Troller Jack forced open the coffin – and you know the rest. Nothing else has been disturbed. It is all perfectly obvious,' Erlandson added with a tone of exasperation.

Faro nodded. 'Possibly so, sir, possibly so. This is purely a matter of routine. There is no disrespect to the deceased intended. And now, we have other work to do. After you, Vince.'

Faro shared his two companions' relief at being in the open air again. It seemed that they all breathed very deeply as they approached the Odin Stone.

It was beginning to rain quite heavily and as he and Vince carefully examined Troller's body they were acutely aware of the minister hovering anxiously in the background. Obviously feeling that his watchful presence ensured that the proprieties were observed with proper reverence, he said, 'When you are finished we will need to move the young man to his home. As soon as possible. His brother will be shocked, quite shocked, poor man.'

Faro looked up sharply. 'Does he not know already? Has no one told him?'

Erlandson shook his head. 'Not unless they could wake him. Regrettably he drinks himself into insensibility rather regularly and can be quite, er, aggressive to anyone who approaches him in that condition. Although I'm informed on the best authority that sober he is gentle as a lamb, I tremble to think how he will react to this dreadful news,' he added with a shudder.

Faro straightened up briefly. 'Since you wish to remain while Dr Laurie examines the body, perhaps you would oblige us with an account of the events leading to the discovery of the two bodies.'

'I have already given Sergeant Frith a full statement,' said Erlandson stiffly.

'Then perhaps you would be so good as to give me another, since I have been left in charge of the case,' Faro said with a winning smile.

Chapter Six

'My bedroom window overlooks the kirkyard.' Erlandson nodded in the direction of the manse. 'I had an upset stomach . . . '

Vince raised his head quickly and looked across at his stepfather who shook his head. He didn't want a comparing of notes with thc minister.

'Miss Balfray, my fiancée, had seen me safely home but, as I felt quite unwell, I slept badly and awoke with a desperate thirst. I got up to get a glass of water.' Hc thought for a moment. 'That would be about two hours ago. It was still dark and I didn't take any heed of the time, but I imagine it would be about five o'clock. The seals were particularly noisy and when I drew the curtains and looked out of the window, I noticed a light down here, flickering beside the vault. I decided to take a look.'

'One moment,' Faro interrupted. 'Was the vault unguarded?'

'So I discovered.'

'Was that not unusual after an interment?'

'We are not as a rule troubled by grave-robbers, and a week-old corpse would be of little use to them. I have little experience of Balfray funerals, or of family vaults,' he added wearily, 'but I understand that the head of the bereaved family normally makes such arrangements as are deemed necessary until the vault is resealed.'

'I see. Continue, if you please.'

Erlandson sighed. 'You know the rest. I was deeply shocked by what I found. I had a quick look at the lad but couldn't rouse him. I'm afraid I put the worst possible interpretation on this. I presumed that he had imbibed too freely. At first. A closer look of course convinced me that he was . . . was—' he shook his head '—quite dead. I didn't know what to do in the circumstances. You must understand I received a terrible shock. Nothing like this has ever happened to me in any of my parishes before. I decided to go for help and as Captain Gibb is nearest to the rectory I aroused him, telling him what had happened. He told me he had seen Sergeant Frith among the mourners and that I should find him. Also, that Dr Balfray must be informed. I ran to the castle, closely followed by Captain Gibb. I am younger than he, and in considerably better condition.'

'You left the Odin Stone unattended. For how long?'

'Half an hour . . . more or less. When I got back Sergeant Frith was examining the body.' Erlandson made an impatient gesture. 'What difference does it make?' he demanded irritably. 'My dear sir, from what I had left here it seemed very unlikely that either of them would get up and walk away.'

And turning his attention again to Vince he watched him examining Troller's head and hands and, with a shudder of distaste, asked, 'Can we now move this poor young man into my vestry until his brother has been notified? He is getting very wet.'

Faro stared at him in mild astonishment. 'We are all getting very wet. I fancy that it will trouble him less than most.' And heeding the minister's sharp intake of breath he added, 'But as you say, it would be an advantage to conduct the rest of our examination indoors.'

'The rest of your examination? Surely you have seen enough? Sergeant Frith is satisfied that this was a suicide.' Erlandson's tone of reproach left them in no doubt that he was considerably shocked by their behaviour thus far.

Vince straightened up. 'I am a doctor, sir, as you know. My thorough medical investigation frequently includes a post-mortem examination of the deceased.'

'A post-mortem? Is that strictly necessary in this case? Really, the distress this will cause . . . '

'Not quite so much distress as has already been caused to this poor young man, sir,' said Vince.

'And I am afraid we are just at the beginning,' Faro added.

'Yes, of course, the funeral . . . '

'There can be no funeral until we have the Procurator Fiscal's report. Whatever Sergeant Frith's findings, I regard the circumstances of this young man's death as highly suspicious. The possibility of foul play cannot be entirely dismissed,' said Faro.

'I have to sign the death certificate and I cannot do so without being quite satisfied about what was the cause of his death,' Vince added sternly.

Erlandson scrutinised Faro carefully, in the manner of one who has been deliberately deceived. 'I heard the sergeant address you as Inspector. How fortunate indeed for my little flock.'

'And now, if you will assist us, sir,' said Vince brusquely. 'This blanket – perhaps we can use it to transport the body to your vestry where we will be reasonably comfortable?'

It was a weary climb to the church supporting their burden. Erlandson unlocked the door of the vestry where Troller's body was placed on a trestle table. Faro's final action of emptying the dead man's pockets, placing on the table a few coins, a pocket knife and a soggy handkerchief brought forth an almost anguished sigh from the minister.

As they left, Faro stretched out his hand for the

key. 'I will take care of that, if you please.' And, as Erlandson regarded him doubtfully, he added, 'In my official capacity.' Erlandson considered the key as if it might be about to express an opinion, before handing it to Faro with a look of gravest suspicion and extreme disapproval.

In the dining room at Balfray Castle, scarcely less grand than its drawing-room, they found Mary Faro's carefully prepared breakfast being completely ignored.

An audience consisting of the entire Balfray family and adherents awaited them with a certain amount of hand-wringing and anxious questions. All were resplendent in mourning for Thora Balfray and looked for all the world, thought Faro grimly, like a set piece for one of Her Majesty's new-fangled group photographs.

Francis Balfray was Vince's chief concern. He looked scarcely more animated than the family portraits on the walls or the corpses they had been investigating. Behind his chair, a newcomer. The woman who stood with her hand protectively on his shoulder was obviously Norma Balfray whom he had glimpsed by the torchlight at the Odin Stone.

Vince was right, she had a certain allure. There was a quality of suppressed passion about her handsome features and Miss Balfray managed to exude sexual attraction remarkably well considering the melancholy circumstances. As they were introduced and she looked deeply into his eyes, Faro thought of the contrast there must have been between the half-sisters. Even allowing for long illness, unfortunate demise and resurrection from the tomb, Thora Balfray in life could never have been counted as a rival.

On the other side of the room, Captain Gibb had apparently collapsed into a chair with Mary Faro hovering anxiously over him.

'Look lively there, lad,' said Faro.

Vince needed no second bidding. He sprang into immediate action, applying one of his instant remedies from his emergency bag. It was perfectly obvious from the man's colour and difficult breathing that if someone didn't do something sharpish then they would have yet another candidate for the kirkyard.

Troller's brother Saul was there, too, seated on a hard chair at a respectful distance from his betters. If looks could be judged then no doubt he was feeling that death would be too good. Red-eyed with shock, he had scarcely emerged from the effects of the night's debauch and was incoherently demanding, 'Wha' ha-happened to Jack?' and 'Don't believe it', almost in the same breath. Sometimes he attempted to spring up, pugnacious in his bewildered grief, and was with difficulty restrained.

Behind his chair stood Inga, her hand on his shoulder. She limited her remarks to 'Hush, hush, my dear' which had little effect on the bereaved sibling.

And hovering in the background was Mary Faro, trying in vain to offer her cups of tea and plates of toast to keep up everyone's strength for the ordeal that lay ahead.

Within moments of entering the room, Vince and Faro were bombarded with frantic but quite relevant questions for which they had not had the least opportunity to prepare satisfactory and consolingly logical answers.

Frith's statement that Troller had fallen down the cliff was being dismissed as a tragic but unfortunate accident, the result of too many drams at the wake. The removal of Mrs Balfray from her coffin was a different matter. A terrible shock, of course, but a situation they were prepared to accept as within the bounds of possibility from a young man of known unsound mind, further unhinged by grief for his beloved patroness.

But no one, thought Faro, had asked Frith how Troller had managed this single-handed, injured as he was, before conveniently expiring at her side. Or, more significantly, what exactly lay behind the Romeo and Juliet death scene so elaborately staged on the Odin Stone?

Erlandson cleared his throat and exercised his ministerial powers by inviting everyone to bow their heads in prayer, a comforting homily Faro recognised as straight from the service for the burial of the dead. This was immediately followed by delicate but practical suggestions for the next few hours.

Faro and Vince left him to it. Erlandson was accustomed to dealing with family bereavement as the vast and elaborate panoply of mourning so firmly established by Her Majesty moved into operation.

'Even on this small island,' Vince told him later, 'the proprieties of death must be observed. Mourning bands for the villagers, wreaths, a church service, black-edged cards, ostrich plumes.'

Could Troller be removed to his own home for the kisting? Saul asked. Vince and Faro exchanged glances. To keep him in the vestry until the Procurator Fiscal arrived would arouse suspicions of foul play. The brother was obviously very distressed but Vince had to explain that they would have to await the arrival of authority.

'Where will they get black ostrich plumes here?' murmured Faro as he and Vince thankfully made their escape.

At the bottom of the staircase, Faro put a finger to his lips and steered Vince in the direction of the front door. He wasn't quick enough. From the dining room emerged Mary Faro, obviously lying in wait for them.

'I thought you two were up to something. I insist that you sit down in my kitchen and have some breakfast before you do anything else and before all the food I've cooked is completely ruined. You must keep your strength up in this hour of trial, Jeremy.'

'We'll be back directly, Mother. Just going for a constitutional. Brisk walk round the grounds.'

Vince grinned at her disarmingly. 'Do us good. Clear our heads. I'll take care of him, Grandma.'

'Sometimes I just think you encourage him. I don't know which of you is worse,' she wailed after them.

Halfway down the drive, Faro said, 'I think we should revisit the scene of the crime. There are one or two small discrepancies we might do well to consider.'

'Deuced awkward having any sort of exchange, let alone a discussion, with the minister breathing so conscientiously down our necks. But I assumed you've noticed them too.'

As they walked rapidly in the direction of the kirkyard, the threatening weather had undergone a further rapid deterioration. Every vestige of late summer had vanished.

Autumn had descended on Balfray and had chosen its day well. The close damp fog clung to houses and covered the ground with an undulating grey blanket of mist. Even as they walked the island had already begun to diminish and landmarks dissolve. With the first deep boom of the foghorn, the seals' lament and a few sheep bleating forlornly were the only indications that life existed beyond their footsteps beneath the growing swirling shroud of grey. The air tasted damp and slightly salty and the prospect before them, as one by one tombstones loomed out of the mist, was anything but beguiling.

'What a day for a murder,' said Faro, burrowing deeper into his coat collar.

Vince surveyed the now deserted Odin Stone bleakly. 'You're absolutely right, Stepfather. Troller wasn't killed by tumbling over the cliff. He was murdered. By a massive blow to the back of his head.'

Chapter Seven

'There is no doubt about it, Stepfather. Troller Jack was also murdered. So we now have two on our hands.'

'One by poisoning and one by a more speedy form of despatch, eh?' said Faro.

'Let's leave Thora Balfray out for the moment because there is a distinct possibility that the two crimes were quite unconnected, don't you agree?'

'I'm curious,' said Faro. 'Everyone I've spoken to thus far has been at great pains to tell me that Balfray is law-abiding, God-fearing, with a highly respected laird. Universal love seems to be the order of the day and murder is unthinkable. Besides, Vince, if you use your powers of observation, you'll note the ground.'

'The ground?'

'Yes, where we are standing now. Come along.'

They walked a few steps and then Faro stopped, kneeled down. 'Look, I'm certain this is where Troller emerged, where he climbed up. See, there are tussocks of grass pulled out, a branch newly broken. Ah, and look on this stone sheltered by the cliff face – dried blood. This is where he dragged himself along. Now follow me.'

As they walked slowly back towards the kirkyard, he continued, 'Observe the ground near the vault. The grass is bruised and there are some impressions, footprints, dammit, most washed away by the rain. Now what does that suggest to you, Vince?'

'Had there been several drunks from the village involved, with a struggle, then there would have been a great many more signs of activity underfoot, trampled ground and so forth.'

'Notice anything odd?' demanded Faro sharply.

Vince frowned. 'When we examined him, it hadn't begun to rain yet his clothes were sodden through – the reason I failed to observe immediately the wound in his matted hair.' He looked across at Faro. 'Also, there was a huge wet patch under him on the Odin Stone although Thora's shroud was bone dry.'

Faro nodded eagerly. 'Very significant. And what else?'

'Where he had been lying, there were pieces of seaweed, particles of sand on his clothes.'

'And what might we conclude from that, I wonder?'

'Obviously he had been in the sea.'

'In the sea?' Faro repeated. 'Doing what? Swimming was hardly likely. Had he fallen in then, do you think? He was drunk, remember, staggering along that narrow cliff path. The question is, did he lose his footing, and fall . . . or was he pushed?

'Inebriates do have miraculous escapes from death, quite unaccountable powers of survival, as we know.'

'Aye, we encounter them in Edinburgh regularly. Everyone was, I gather, maudlin drunk at the wake including our off-duty Sergeant Frith.'

'It could happen, you know. Troller was physically very strong, in the prime of condition. It was only his poor brain that was weak. And the shock of contact with icy water might well have sobered him.'

'Let us presume that you are right. So with nothing more than a drenching and a few bruises, he climbs up again, tearing his hands while his wet garments gather quantities of mud, sand and seaweed.'

Faro shook his head. 'We have missed one very

significant fact, lad. Why make that tortuous dangerous climb at all? Ah, there's the rub.' Turning, he pointed a finger to the way they had come. 'When there is a perfectly good path only thirty yards away leading up from the shore? And why, instead of going home by that path, sobered and grateful for his miraculous escape, does he further risk life and limb to trot off to Thora's tomb—?'

'Oblivious of a deep wound on the back of his head which was to cause his death,' Vince interrupted. 'It just isn't feasible, Stepfather. Whatever he did do, concussed, bleeding profusely, he certainly didn't make that climb with a split skull and then take Thora from her coffin and carry her, unaided, to that other resting place.'

'Without knowing the full facts of the case, I would say that the murderous attack took place, either before or after putting Mrs Balfray on the Odin Stone.'

'And if before, Stepfather, we can only come to one conclusion. That someone else arranged their particularly grisly death scene.'

Faro shivered, listening to the floodtide biting deep into the rocks far below, and all around them the heavy swathe of mist blanketing the landscape and reducing visibility to nil.

'Someone from the village, would you say? Some of the lads who tormented him and were the worse for drink at the wake?'

'Unlikely,' said Vince. 'From all accounts, Troller was well thought of and Saul Hoy is a mighty force to be reckoned with, enough to discourage anyone with a cruel and senseless line in practical joking.'

'Excellent. So you would agree that we direct our enquiries closer to home to find the answer to this one. You know the first rules by now, lad, without any prompting from me.'

Vince smiled. 'You mean motive.'

'Precisely. Let us first consider who stood to gain by Troller's death.'

'I can answer that, Stepfather. No one. The lad was an orphan. Only Saul Hoy stood to gain . . . '

'Indeed?'

'By having one less mouth to feed,' Vince replied grimly. 'And that's a callous assessment for, according to everyone, Saul was devoted to his simple brother. And I think we'll find he didn't even have an insurance on him which might have made him only a few pounds richer or would pay for the funeral wake.'

They had reached the Balfray vault. 'Let's go inside, shall we?'

Vince followed him reluctantly, obviously regarding with distaste a prospect only minutely more daunting than the weather outside.

As Faro lit the lantern and lifted the coffin lid they both took a step back at the chilling odour of death.

'We know that Troller was in the sea, for what reason it isn't yet clear. But when he reached Thora's tomb . . . did you notice that it was quite dry inside, immaculately tidy, in fact? There were no wet marks, no sand or seaweed, as you would imagine from a man whose clothes were dripping wet.'

Faro lifted the lantern so that its light illuminated the coffin. 'Now what sort of implement did he use to unscrew the lid?'

'The pocket knife we found in his pocket would have been quite adequate.'

Vince shuddered as Faro paced across the vault carrying an imaginary burden. 'So, he takes out Mrs Balfray and carries her to the Odin Stone.' Turning, he regarded his stepson gravely. 'What were his reasons for such extraordinary behaviour, do you think?'

Vince frowned. 'Are we to believe he was still fuddled enough with drink to imagine that the stone had powers to resurrect dead lovers?'

Faro smiled. 'Ah, now you are getting close, lad, for that is precisely what we are meant to believe.' Frowning, he added, 'But was that all he intended? There is another highly unpleasant possibility, which I expect has already occurred to you.'

'Necrophilia, you mean?'

'The same. Perhaps by the light of an indifferent moon.'

Vince looked shocked. 'I think you are quite mistaken. I'm sure his love was absolutely pure for Thora.'

'In moments of sanity and sobriety, yes. But mad drunk . . . he had the mind of a child, Vince, but his body was that of a young and virile man. So who knows what desires overwhelmed him when he opened that coffin?'

'You're wrong, Stepfather. We both saw Thora's corpse. Her grave-clothes weren't even disarranged . . . '

Faro smiled. 'Exactly. They were remarkably well starched – pristine, in fact.' Leaning forward, he added, 'Observe closely the satin lining of the coffin.'

With a certain repugnance Vince looked over his stepfather's shoulder in the lantern light. 'Not a stain there, either, of any kind.'

'Nor was there any such mark when we replaced her. Now, does that not strike you as remarkable?'

'It does indeed since the blood on his hands had not yet congealed when we found him,' said Vince.

'Yet, considering the frightful condition of Troller's person, not so much as a spot of mud or blood, not even a peck of sand on Mrs Balfray, who he must have clasped quite firmly in his arms to negotiate the narrow door and the steps up from the vault.'

Faro smiled grimly. 'And what does he do next?

He arranges her on the Odin Stone, lies down and conveniently expires beside her.'

Vince shook his head. 'Whatever impulse, pure or impure, drove him, I don't believe a word of it.'

'And neither do I,' said Faro, thumping his fists together. 'Not a single word.'

'Do you think we have seen enough in here?' said Vince anxiously. Even in the lantern glow, Faro observed that he was beginning to look a little green, the effect of holding his breath for long intervals.

'For the present, yes.' And closing the coffin lid, Faro gratefully followed his stepson into the moist air. After wiping their faces with handkerchiefs, they sat down on the steps and Faro lit a pipe.

'Most distressing, most distressing, this whole business. And, alas, I fear there will be worse to come . . . '

'If Troller didn't perform these miraculous feats, then who staged the dramatic death scene?'

'Someone deuced anxious to make it look as if there was a connection.' Faro shook his head. 'Find the answer to that, lad, and we have our murderer. Let's not be blinded by the obvious, and keep always in sight the vital question – motive, lad, concentrate on that. Find out who had motive and opportunity, and we're halfway there.'

'Who should want to destroy a harmless simpleton, liked by everyone?'

'Precisely. Let us presume that the two deaths are connected and that whoever murdered Thora Balfray had good reason for wanting rid of Troller.'

'Such as?'

'Let us say that he had stumbled on something important – the identity of Mrs Balfray's murderer.'

'It's a fantastic theory, Stepfather, but you could be right.'

Faro was silent for a moment before replying. 'There

is another alternative. That Troller's murder was an accident.'

'An accident?'

'Let's leave aside for a moment his maudlin love for Thora Balfray. Picture instead a very frightened murderer – on the verge of being discovered. Only in such dire necessity would he, or she, have resorted to this quite unplanned violence.'

'He or she,' Vince repeated. 'But it must have been a man, Stepfather. No woman could ever have grappled with Thora's corpse.'

'Difficult, I admit, but not impossible.' Faro paused. 'Not for a woman used to lifting a sick person in her bed over several months.'

'Of course. You have something there,' said Vince triumphantly. 'Why didn't I think of that before? Hospital nurses tell me there's a knack in it.' And, with a look of faint horror, he added, 'You mean . . . ?'

'Well, perhaps it is a little far-fetched, a little early for that. Let's concentrate on the likelihood of a man being involved, on our earlier theory of the murderer waiting for Troller when he staggered up the cliff path and attacking him with a heavy implement that split open his skull and, I suspect, killed him instantly.'

'What did he use?'

Faro looked around. 'In all probability whatever was nearest and most effective for the job. In these surroundings, with an unplanned attack, I'd hazard a guess that he'd use a spade. There are always plenty lurking about kirkyards, the natural implement for digging graves. I dare say it isn't far away.'

As Faro spoke he walked rapidly towards the tiny woodshed where the grave diggers kept the tools of their trade. A moment later he gave a cry of triumph.

'This, I think, is our murder weapon. See for yourself.' He held up a spade for Vince's inspection.

'By heaven, you're right, Stepfather. Blood stains . . . and hair on the blade.'

They were silent, struck by the enormity of what they had discovered. The murder weapon between them, they were isolated in a gloomy kirkyard where all contact with life had long since ceased and even the comfort of horizons had vanished. Their range of vision was now limited to a few yards, bound by swirling shadows of heavy vapour, shrouding the church and turning the tombstones into the shapes of lurking ghosts.

Suddenly it was not a place in which to linger. With only the echoes of the seals barking, Faro was seized by an ominous feeling that this was one case he was never going to solve. Defeated already, a fit of sneezing did nothing to lessen his depression.

Vince looked at him anxiously. He knew the signs well. 'Cheer up, Stepfather, a good hot bath is the answer. And that, thanks to the ingenuity of Balfray plumbing, can be instantly provided.'

Chapter Eight

An hour later, Faro sat in front of a large fire in his bedroom, wrapped in a bathrobe. Under the disapproving eye of Mrs Faro, Vince generously replenished their whisky glasses.

Mrs Faro raised her eyes heavenward, frustrated that the management of her son's health on which she prided herself had been entirely removed from under her ample wing. Drams, except for high days and holidays, she regarded as instruments of the devil.

As he sipped his drink, Faro unashamedly encouraged her to tell him all about Balfray. She was not unwilling and a lively interest in local gossip was exactly what he most needed, with an idea that Mrs Faro's ear for seemingly irrelevant information could be of considerable importance.

He soon got more than he had bargained for and found his eyelids drooping under a barrage of life histories of the entire population of Balfray but was, in effect, only the staff inside and out, past and present, of Balfray Castle.

'Poor as church mice they are. That poor Miss Balfray, she has such a job making ends meet.'

Faro's head sank a little lower.

'Paid off most of the servants. All new now except Annie.'

Faro jerked awake. 'Who's Annie?'

'Haven't you been listening, dear? Annie, the upper

housemaid, has been with them since before Dr Francis married.'

'And everyone else is new?'

She smiled reproachfully. 'Like I've just told you, dear.'

Faro was fully alert again as he made a mental note to talk to Annie. Why should this complete change of servants bother him? Had it been coincidence, as his mother claimed, or was there some carefully thought out pattern behind it all – a sinister reason that might be connected with the two deaths?

When Mrs Faro took her departure full of anxious concern and advice for his future well-being, Faro felt considerably more cheerful.

Vince settled himself comfortably in the opposite armchair. 'Do you get an odd feeling that we might have dreamed the last few hours, Stepfather?'

'I wish we had, Vince, since it now appears without much shadow of a doubt that we have two murders to consider.'

'I've been thinking. And, since it is highly unlikely that Troller's death was for any motive of gain, the connection between the two deaths does seem rather far-fetched, don't you agree?'

Faro did not reply. A moment later, he said, 'Francis Balfray – let us consider him, shall we?'

'As far as he knows his wife died of natural causes . . . '

'Pneumonia as a result of chronic malnutrition occasioned by gastric disorders. Was that what you wrote on the death certificate?' Faro watched his stepson wince.

'Not quite. Of pneumonia and heart failure brought about by the effects of a long debilitating disease.'

'Who was with her at the end?'

'Francis, Norma and myself.'

Faro stared into the fire. 'And only Francis stood to gain by Thora's death?'

'As I've told you, Stepfather. There are no other heirs.'

'A pity, since they have been married for several years.'

'Three to be precise. Presumably they still hoped for an heir, before Thora's illness.'

'And if Francis should die, then, and only then, will all his wife's fortune go to her stepsister,' Faro repeated slowly.

'I'm told that Norma and she were the last of their line, the last direct link with the Balfrays who had been on the island since the fourteenth century.'

'What about heirs in that cadet branch of Gibb's?' Faro demanded.

'You would have to ask Francis or the Captain the answer to that.'

Faro rubbed his chin thoughtfully. 'I still want to know what made Francis choose the younger plainer sister.'

'Thora had a very sweet nature, very loving and trusting.' Vince did not sound altogether convinced and Faro smiled.

'I've seen her wedding photograph in the drawing-room. To be more practical than romantic, let us admit that her fortune was sweeter than her face. It's an old, old story, lad.'

'We are being cynical and cruel,' said Vince. 'Poor Francis, I don't know how he is going to take the news of Thora's poisoning in his present condition, and to learn that we have a murderer in our midst.'

Observing his stepfather's expression, he added in awed tones, 'You can't possibly suspect Francis?'

Faro ignored the question. 'He was laird of Balfray, it was as good as his. He had achieved his great ambition, so why the devil didn't he marry Norma?'

'From what I've told you already, and Grandma has confirmed it,' said Vince in tones of slight exasperation at his stepfather's persistence, 'Balfray estate is nothing but unpaid bills, and a vast upkeep which Norma is finding very hard to manage, even with the help, or hindrance, of Captain Gibb as factor.'

'What makes you think he might be a hindrance?'

'An old sea-dog, as he calls himself, can't be much of a hand with the pennies, do you think?'

'That depends. I imagine that managing finances on a Navy ship would be in the hands of the purser, but if it was a merchantman . . .'

'He calls himself Navy retired.'

Faro's shrug was expressive and Vince continued, 'To get back to Francis, if you're hinting that he might have planned to marry Norma after getting rid of Thora and inheriting her fortune, I don't think that's feasible. And I doubt whether marriage with a deceased wife's sister is permissible in the Episcopalian Church.'

Faro frowned. 'Norma Balfray's motive could have been a little more primitive, a festering human emotion.'

'Jealousy, you mean. Highly improbable as she is going to marry John Erlandson.'

Faro smiled grimly. 'And betrothals, as we have seen, can be broken. How did Francis react to their announcement?'

'He was delighted. Erlandson was well received and, I gather, greatly welcomed by Francis as a future member of the family. As for Thora, she approved heartily of the match, happy for her stepsister who had found happiness at last— '

'In spite of her own actions.'

Vince ignored the interruption. 'Found happiness in such an unexpected quarter. Who could have guessed that the new minister would be attractive and eligible in every way as an eminently suitable husband for Miss Balfray?'

Faro was silent as he poked the fire into bright

embers. 'So only if Francis were to die now would Norma inherit Thora's fortune.' He looked across at his stepson. 'I think we shall have to watch Francis closely, very closely indeed.'

'You think he might be in danger?' asked Vince in tones of alarm.

Faro shrugged. 'Well, it seems that he has already been threatened. And the prankster with the cloak on the cliff path might be more successful next time.'

With the rapidity that marked changes of weather in the islands, the mists and rain suddenly vanished to leave a sky innocent and benign, as if the presence of a single cloud had never threatened its vast and endless blue.

Vince looked out of the window approvingly. 'The boat from Kirkwall is due in shortly. Francis' dispensary is alarmingly run down and while he is temporarily out of action, I should hate to have to deal with some emergency.'

'I should come with you and visit the Procurator Fiscal,' said Faro with a certain lack of enthusiasm.

Vince smiled. Looks deceived and despite Faro's impressive Viking bearing and island ancestry, he had a regrettable tendency to seasickness, especially when faced with small boats on large seas.

'I shouldn't advise it. Sergeant Frith won't thank you for pulling rank on him.'

Faro looked suitably contrite. 'Would you do something else for me? Go into the newspaper office and ask them if they can oblige with any reports of mysterious accidents, drownings and so forth, over the last year.'

Vince gave him a puzzled look.

'It's just a hunch, lad. There may be a connecting link somewhere else in the islands. A pattern which will give us some clues.'

Sitting at the window he began what he called his

dramatis personae of Balfray Island, pausing to wave to Vince and Mrs Faro walking down the drive together. The presence of a laden basket on his mother's arm betokened a visit to one of her many waifs and strays.

As he wrote each name he pondered which, however innocently, might be in possession of some thread that led through the labyrinth. To the list, he added one more name: 'Mrs Bliss?' Was he investigating two murders – or could it be three? What if Mrs Bliss's unfortunate drowning had not been an accident, but the one that had begun it all?

Throwing down his pen and guessing that his mother might be absent for some time, he decided this was an excellent chance to visit the kitchen and talk to the maid Annie.

At that moment the door opened to admit a uniformed maid, with an island woman's rosy cheeks and ample girth.

'Sorry, sir, I thought you were out.' She indicated the bucket she carried. 'Missus told me I was to be sure and put more peats on your fire.'

Missus could only be his mother and Faro smiled. 'You must be Annie?' A nod indicated that this was so. 'I understand from Mrs Faro that you are a great help to her, that she would be quite lost without you.'

Annie beamed. 'Missus is very kind to everyone. I expect it's because she's one of us.' And with an apologetic look added, 'Belongs to the islands, I mean, so she knows all our peedie ways.'

'Have you been at the castle long?'

'Going on ten years, sir.'

'You must have seen a lot of changes then?'

'Oh yes, sir. I was here when Sir Joseph was alive, Miss Balfray's father.'

'Miss Balfray?' Faro frowned innocently. 'That would be before she married Dr Francis?'

'Oh no, sir, you've got it wrong. Not her that is gone – her stepsister, Miss Norma Balfray, although we all thought once that it was her Dr Francis was to marry . . . '

And Faro found himself listening to a tale he knew well already and which lost nothing of its domestic drama in the telling, of Dr Balfray's surprising change of heart. Such goings-on had obviously been a matter of eager gossip and speculation in the kitchen.

'You don't seem to have many servants,' he interposed at last. 'How do you manage?'

'Oh fine, sir. There's not all that much work unless we have guests. When her that has gone, God rest her, was taken ill, there was no more entertaining at the castle.'

She stopped and looked at him earnestly. 'We all help each other out, you see. If help is needed in the house, we can always get someone in from the village.'

'How do the bachelor gentlemen manage?'

'You mean the minister and Captain Gibb?'

'Yes, do they have servants of their own?'

Annie shook her head. 'Not living in. The Captain said he had no call for a woman about the house. He was used to doing for himself on his ship.' She smiled. 'A typical old sailor, the Captain. As for Reverend Erlandson, my cousin Bessie, who cleans the church, cooks his meals and keeps the rectory tidy. I dare say when he and Miss Balfray marry there'll be a different arrangement then.'

'A housekeeper, perhaps?'

Annie frowned. 'Housekeepers are hard to keep on Balfray, sir, as Missus may have told you.'

'Because of Mrs Bliss's unfortunate accident, perhaps?'

Annie shuffled her feet and regarded them solemnly, searching for the right words, he thought.

'She wasn't one of us, sir, she didn't know the island ways. She never realised how we all rely on each other. Sometimes she was, well, selfish, thoughtless.'

Annie permitted herself a grim smile. 'She liked going into Kirkwall and meeting people. She did like the gentlemen,' she added delicately and then closed her mouth firmly in the manner of one who has already said too much.

Faro was saved from further probing by the entrance of Miss Balfray. 'I thought I heard your voice, Annie, gossiping again. Oh, Mr Faro, I didn't realise.'

As Annie scuttled out with a brief curtsy, Norma Balfray said, 'I hope everyone is looking after you. We are, I'm afraid, a little short on hospitality at this particular time.'

As he assured her of his well-being, he was conscious of the intensity of her gaze. For once he found himself at a disadvantage, searching for the kind of conversation that usually came so easily to him.

Next morning, the real motive behind Norma's most pressing concern regarding his presence at Balfray still troubled him as, beguiled by the sunshine, he walked briskly towards the cliff path.

With a feeling that all his senses were sharpened by this brilliant light and a gleaming sea, he was not without hope of perhaps stumbling upon some small clue that they had previously overlooked.

However, as he walked towards the sea wood he found that he was not alone. A girl emerged from one of the paths.

No, not a girl. It was Inga St Ola.

Chapter Nine

'May I walk with you? I feel a need to escape too on such a lovely morning,' Inga added sympathetically.

It wasn't quite what Faro had intended. They walked in a silence he found both companionable and oddly comforting while he considered what useful information he might extract regarding Balfray and its occupants.

Suddenly Inga said, 'I expect you've heard about Saul Hoy?'

When he shook his head innocently, she smiled. 'Come along, Jeremy. It's common talk – I'm the speak of Balfray, as they say in these parts, living all these years with a bachelor who is not my husband.'

She sighed. 'Saul's a good man, and I expect I would have married him, if he hadn't turned out to be my half-brother.'

Faro wondered why he felt so pleased when she added, 'We've been very happy in our brother–sister relationship. Living with Saul has protected me from occasional outbursts – when a cow dies, or someone fancies she is being overlooked by a selkie, sometimes they've come to do me violence . . . '

She stopped, her eyes narrowing suddenly, as if reliving such incidents with painful clarity. 'But when they find they have Saul to deal with, it's a different story. Having a protector can be very useful, as I've discovered.'

'I gather your Saul Hoy was devoted to his younger brother too.'

'He was. But as for poor Troller, no one else existed in his world except Thora Balfray. It's sad that he died, but I think his life was over the very day she breathed her last.'

'His death was very strange, bizarre even. You must have known him better than most. Have you any theories of your own as to what happened?'

Inga shrugged. 'Only what Frith said. Poor Troller set off with some insane idea that he could bring his beloved Mrs Balfray back to life. On the way in the dark he lost his balance, took a tumble down the cliff. He climbed up again, put Thora on the Odin Stone but when its magical powers didn't take effect, well, he decided to end it all.'

'How?' demanded Faro sharply. 'By what means? You're not presuming that his injuries were enough to kill him?'

She looked at him, as if bewildered by the question. 'Perhaps, perhaps not. In his distraught condition, he might have helped matters along, taken poison, always accessible to a handyman on the estate.'

'You mean, he had it with him, just in case? What sort of poison had you in mind?'

'Oh for heaven's sake, Jeremy,' she said irritably. 'I don't know.' Then, mollified by his expression, she added, 'Probably arsenic, there's plenty of it about.'

'Is there indeed? Where do they buy it?'

'Kirkwall, and Stromness too, I believe.'

'Are we to presume they also sign the poisons register?'

Inga shook her head, laughing. 'You may presume what you like, my dear Inspector Faro, but I don't think anyone sets much store on signing registers here. It's not as if it was being asked for by strangers, just the local folk, known to all the shopkeepers as having trouble with vermin and the like.'

'Interesting.'

She gave him a hard look before continuing, 'Everyone here uses arsenic at some time or other. Killing rats or on flypapers – flies are cruel in the summer.' In a gesture that was becoming endearingly familiar, she pushed back her hair from her forehead. 'Why is it so important, Jeremy?' she added softly.

He could not risk telling her that Troller had been murdered, as had Thora. Ignoring the question, he said, 'My mother tells me you've been indispensable these last few weeks.'

Inga looked pleased. 'And so has she. Absolute marvel. The way she stepped into poor Mrs Bliss's shoes.'

Taking her arm, he led her down the steep and winding path that led to the shore, a wide expanse of empty beach broken by occasional large rock formations. The tide was out and rock pools gleamed full of coloured stones and red sea-anemones.

Once Inga stopped and climbed across a tiny wall of ancient stones. 'Do you realise that this was once the foundation of someone's house? Long, long ago. Who they were and where they went has been washed away, lost for ever under the sea.'

She indicated a place beside her on a large flat stone and together they contemplated the vast loneliness of the scene, the great stretch of shell sand uninterrupted into the far distance where the lighthouse was the only habitation.

Above their heads the sky was strangely empty of seabirds, the seals having temporarily deserted their rocks. Now only a few sheep grazed among the seaweed left by the tide.

'You'll find this hard to believe, Jeremy, but had you sat here even six months ago, the scene would have been quite different.'

'Indeed? It looks to me as if it's been here since the beginning of time.'

Inga shook her head. 'Not so. The sea is so strong, it moves sand and shingle with such rapidity and in such a short time that the miles of shoreline are completely altered and every year landmarks, huge stones that have been used for years and years as anchorage for boats, completely vanish almost overnight. Landmarks long forgotten just as suddenly reappear from under the sea, like this house wall we're sitting on.'

'Remarkable.'

'Remarkable it is. It gives living on a small island a feeling of impermanence. Once this place must have teemed with life, Jeremy. But we are at the mercy of the sea and we must never forget it. We are constantly reminded that we must honour and do reverence to the sea and fear it. Never, never take it for granted,' she added solemnly.

Faro looked at the stretch of sand before them and lit his pipe, smiling at her as he did so. 'I take it we are safe enough here for a few moments.'

There was no answering smile. 'As long as you know the tide times, yes. But never come here at floodtide.'

'Like the unfortunate housekeeper?'

'Poor Mrs Bliss,' she sighed.

'What happened exactly?' Faro asked innocently, curious to hear Inga's version of the accident, which turned out to be exactly what he had heard already. With one addition.

'I was the one who found her,' said Inga. 'It was horrible. I sometimes come down to collect special specimens of seaweed, for some of my herbal remedies,' she explained. 'And there she was, lying at the tide edge.' She shuddered. 'I knew at once that she was dead, still clinging to poor peedie Waifie.'

'Waifie?'

'Yes, her dog . . . that had caused it all.'

'Had she been missing long?'

'She'd been away from the castle overnight, we learned afterwards.'

'Had no one thought of searching for her?'

'They didn't know she had gone out after the dog until John Erlandson said he'd heard her shouting its name and asked him if he'd seen it. And we didn't know that until afterwards.'

Inga stopped speaking for a moment. 'It was very near here, where I found her. Poor Mrs Bliss. If only someone had realised when she didn't go back to the castle.'

'Wasn't anyone at all concerned enough to look for her when she didn't appear that evening?'

Inga shook her head. 'No. I gather she was a law unto herself, her own boss. Made her own rules did Mrs Bliss. Used to vanish into Kirkwall or even further afield. So Annie, who was left in charge, told everyone later. It all came out then, how she neglected her duties, but, knowing how hard it is to get a reliable housekeeper on an island the size of Balfray, I expect she felt free to take liberties.'

Faro made sympathetic noises. 'What sort of a woman was she?'

Inga smiled. 'Nice enough. And very well bred. She had obviously been trained in high service. But not nearly as efficient as your mother,' she added quickly.

'Middle-aged, was she?' he said.

'Good heavens, no. Thirty, thirty-five at most. Handsome woman, well set up.'

'Indeed. I got the impression that all housekeepers were homely and stout.'

Inga laughed. 'Not this one. Do you know, I even suspected that Saul had an eye on her at one time. And a good thing that would have been.'

She stopped. 'Incidentally, your mother's good spring-cleaning discovered cupboards that had been overlooked for some time and she found a tin box belonging to Mrs Bliss. She didn't know what to do with it, full of papers, references and so forth, I think.'

'Where is it now?'

'I have it at Saul's.'

'Didn't any relatives come to the funeral?'

'After she died so suddenly we couldn't find any address of relatives, or next of kin. She hinted that she was alone in the world. But not, apparently, if the name Mr Leon Bliss in her notebook we found was anything to go by.'

'Mr Leon Bliss?'

Inga shrugged. 'Probably her estranged husband, poor soul.'

'Nothing in this notebook to give any clues?'

'Just recipes and so forth. Dr Balfray decided that Mr Bliss must be a relative and wrote to him at the address on one of her references. However, Norma said the letter came back "Not known".'

'Perhaps she was a widow or the Mrs was a courtesy title.'

Inga shrugged. 'I gather she wasn't exactly forthcoming about her life before Balfray.'

'I'd like to have a look at the contents of that tin box sometime.'

Inga laughed. 'Just curiosity? Or a challenge the inspector cannot resist, is that it?'

Faro smiled. 'Something like that.' Holding out his hand he raised her to her feet and she threw away the stick with which she had been idly making patterns in the sand as they talked.

It was a habit he remembered. But once upon a time those patterns had been hearts with their names elaborately produced and entwined. Now all she had written in the sand was 'Bliss'. The name of a woman dead as their own love.

Chapter Ten

Inga's suggestion that he meet Saul Hoy offered Faro the chance he was looking for, to begin his investigations informally. And who better to give him information than the murdered boy's brother?

The utmost tact would be called for, but he was a past master at conducting such revealing interviews without a hint that there was anything like murder involved.

'Tell them there's been a murder or a serious crime and at once they'll close up like coffin lids,' he once warned his colleagues at Edinburgh's Central Office.

To Inga he said, 'Yes, I should like to pay my condolences.'

The tiny garden attached to the smithy was neat and tidy, much more feminine than he had imagined, until he realised it had been cherished by Inga's green fingers for some years past.

Bees hummed over the herb garden and the perfume of sweet-smelling herbs threw him into a confusion of memories. Thyme he recognised from his childhood, green sage and basil.

Closing the gate, Inga broke off a strand of rosemary and handed it to him. A gesture from a summer long past, and twenty years slipped into oblivion as if they had never been apart. Closing his eyes, he inhaled the herb's heady fragrance, twirling it between his fingers.

Following Inga across the threshold, he realised the interior of the tiny cottage was typical of Inga herself.

There was none of the spartan-like surroundings which typified the crofter's house in Orkney. Only the rich had stone-built mansions. The poor lived in hovels and those hovels were desperately bleak places inside. But here the walls held ornamentation, not practical pots and pans battered by constant use. Here there were samplers, texts whose comforting simplicity and worthy sentiments matched the large smithy kitchen with its uneven stone floor and walls, whitewashed to hide the scars of two hundred years.

On either side of the fire, two hooded Orkney chairs, a colourful rag rug on the floor between them. A huge dresser displayed a collection of blue and white plates, while china figures graced mantelpiece and windowsills where late roses bloomed in vases with a mixture of herbs whose fragrance pervaded the room.

Gesturing him towards a chair, Inga moved a half-knitted sock and placed it in a basket of home-dyed wool. Was it for Saul, Faro wondered enviously, with a sudden stab of longing that it might be himself who was the recipient.

As Inga stirred the fire's embers and set the kettle to boil, he considered that imagination rendered no greater contrast possible between the red inferno next door, with its continual ringing of hammer on forge and the smell of burning hooves, and this room. A room that begged the stranger to rest and be comfortable and invited the exchange of confidences over the tantalising odours of fresh baked bere bannocks.

There was inexpressible delight in these four walls, indefinable magic, Faro thought, as if all the warmth and love that Inga had been unable to put into marriage and raising a family had been lavished into a cottage, full of tender warmth, homemaking skills and healing of body and spirit.

He had taken no more than a sip of tea when Saul

Hoy clattered down the narrow wooden stair, towel in hand. His giant frame, mophead of unruly white curls, black beard and gaunt appearance were considerably improved by recent ablutions. Only about his fine dark eyes the haunted images of the night seemed to cling, as if therein the horrors of the past few hours were still reflected. As the two men shook hands, Inga tactfully withdrew to bring in more peat for the fire.

Saul came to the point quickly. 'Why won't they let me have the laddie's body? Reverend Erlandson tells me that I have to ask you for permission to have him home for the kisting. And what's all this business about getting the Fiscal over?' he demanded irritably.

Faro explained that this was the usual procedure in any case where the death certificate could not be signed as 'natural causes', which included those who took their own lives.

'Where do you fit into all this, mister?'

'I'm a policeman,' said Faro simply. He wasn't prepared to lie or evade. The truth would have to come out sometime.

'Oh, a policeman,' Saul repeated suspiciously. 'I thought you was just on a holiday.'

'So I was . . . and am. Policemen take holidays like everyone else, you know, and I wanted to visit my mother and my bairns.'

Saul's expression softened. 'She's a good woman, your mother. An angel to everyone, she is. She was good to the laddie, too.' Suddenly he sprang to his feet and looked down on Faro with an undisguised air of menace.

Shaking his head from side to side like a demented creature maddened by pain, he shouted, 'You'll never get me to believe the laddie took his own life! Never. He wasn't like that. As for that business— ' he made a disgusted grimace ' —of taking Mrs Balfray from her coffin and . . . and . . . lying down beside her. Such a thought would never have occurred to him. She was sacred to him. He never as much as took her hand when she was alive. As for touching her when she was dead . . . ' Saul's eyes widened in horrified disgust. 'God, he thought the world of her, but he respected her so much that he would have been sick at the thought of anyone touching her.'

Faro was interested to realise that despite his protests about his simple brother Troller, the idea of necrophilia had occurred to the blacksmith too.

'Mrs Balfray belonged to a different world, see. There's them, and a long way down the ladder there's us.'

At Faro's doubtful look, he prodded the air with his finger. 'If you don't believe me, ask any of the estate folk and they'd tell you the same. It would be like . . . like— ' he tried to find the word ' —blasphemy. Yes, blasphemy, to lay a hand on the laird's wife.'

There was a delicate pause before Faro said, 'There was then nothing carnal in your brother's devotion to Mrs Balfray?'

'Carnal?' Saul thought about the word and what it might mean before shaking his head vigorously. 'If you mean he wanted to . . . to bed with her – no. She was a goddess to him. Like I said.'

And, leaning forward, his face inches from Faro's own, 'What you don't seem to realise, mister, was that Troller was still a child, a peedie bairn for all his man's body. He thought like an eight-year-old. And it's the thoughts that count. You can ask Inga, too, if you don't believe me.'

After a pause Faro said, 'Tell me about the night when you last saw him.'

'To be honest with you, I don't mind much of the last hours. We all had that much to eat and drink, a regular funeral wake it was, laird did us proud. The drams flowing . . . '

'Did your brother indulge too?' was Faro's tactful question.

'He did not. He stayed sober as a judge. Aye, at one stage,' he added sheepishly, 'I remember urging him to take more drams, to cheer him up like. But he wasn't having any, shrugged me off, turned his back on us all and just sat there, the poor lad, looking lost and sad.'

'When did you leave this gathering? What time was it?'

'How do I know that, mister? Who keeps count of time when folks are enjoying themselves? All I remember was that sometime, Troller was worried about me, shaking me by the shoulder, trying to wake me up. I can still see his face . . . oh God!'

He covered his face with his hands and sobbed, 'Oh, the poor laddie. He was that concerned about me. He said he was going home and that I should come with him while I was still able to walk.'

With a violent shake of his head, he added, 'And that was true enough, for no man could carry me single-handed. He managed to get me to the door of the hall, saying the fresh air would do me good. But I wasn't having any. I pushed him away. Told him to go home on his own if he liked, I wasn't ready to leave.'

He stopped and stared out of the window, frowning. 'All I remember is seeing him going across the road and down towards the cliff path. He was walking slowly, shaking his head, talking to himself, as he did when he was sad. So sad he was, poor laddie.'

'He was alone?'

'When Troller was sad, he always wanted to be off on his own. Like a sick animal.'

'Why did he go down the cliff path?'

'He loved the seals. Said they talked to him. Even as a peedie bairn if he was upset he'd go down and tell them his troubles.'

Saul sobbed again. 'Oh God forgive me. If I hadn't

drink taken, I might have gone with him, let him take me home and none of this would have ever happened.'

'What do you think happened?'

'Isn't that obvious to anyone, mister? Why, he was talking to the seals, just like always, when he missed his footing and rolled down the cliff and into the sea. His clothes were soaking wet, Reverend Erlandson said, and all seaweedy when he found him on that stone.'

'You believe it would have been possible for him to fall down the cliff and into the sea without doing himself any harm?'

Saul looked surprised. 'Yes. Why not?'

'Well, one would imagine that he – any man – would have received dreadful injuries in the fall and would have been rendered incapable of climbing back up the cliff, as he apparently did.'

Saul sighed and shook his head. 'But Troller wasn't any man, mister. He was a very strong lad . . . ' Stifling a sob, he continued, 'Poor laddie, poor laddie, when he climbed back up, he just didn't realise how badly he'd been hurt, his head cut and all. I reckon he felt a bit groggy-kind and decided to lie down and take a rest on the Odin Stone. There he collapsed and . . . and . . . passed away.'

Faro was silent, seeking the right words. 'Do you think there was any possibility that someone followed him that night?'

'Followed him? You mean, to do him harm?'

'There is that possibility. Someone drunk, wanting to frighten him,' he added awkwardly.

Saul laughed harshly. 'Not on this island. Everyone thought the world of Troller. And I'll tell you one thing, they'll be just as keen as I am to see justice done and his name cleared. So, Mr Policeman, anything you can do will be greatly appreciated.'

Leaning forward, he shook a large fist in Faro's

face. 'Someone else put Mrs Balfray beside him and when I find the bastard who did that to my brother, I'll kill him,' he added ferociously.

Faro left with a very clear picture in his mind now of the first part of the puzzle, that prelude to murder. The simple Troller walking down the cliff path, as he had done a thousand times before in his life, for his lone vigil with the seals. Perhaps they knew the answer, the only ones who saw what really happened and could never tell.

'Jeremy!'

It was Inga hurrying towards him, wrapping a shawl about her shoulders. 'Thank you for spending so much time with Saul. It will have helped him, I know, to have you to talk to,' she added breathlessly. 'My goodness, you do walk quickly.'

He smiled. 'Especially when I'm thinking.'

'You always did that.' Her smile was tender, the words spoken softly. There was a short silence and, almost embarrassed now, her tone brusque, she said, 'Well, is there anything I can tell you?'

'You were at the wake?'

'Until the end. And I had a clear head. I never touch the stuff.'

'So you would have seen if Troller had got into any disagreement with anyone . . . anything like that?'

She stopped walking, staring down at the sea. 'It's like Saul told you, Jeremy. Troller didn't have an enemy in the world. Besides, they would have Saul to reckon with – physically he's the strongest man on the island.' They walked in silence and then she said, 'Poor Troller, that climb, injured as he was and then taking Thora out of her coffin. The effort must have been too much for his poor heart. He just lay down and died. There just isn't any other explanation, whatever Saul wants us to believe.'

Faro considered her thoughtfully. Interesting that she had abandoned the arsenic theory.

'Besides, none of the young folk except Troller would dare walk down the cliff path when the moon is full and the seal king is on the rampage,' she added firmly.

'They surely don't believe that, Inga, this is 1871 . . . '

'1871 or 1371 – it's all the same to them. They believe that the seal king takes human form and steals a mortal bride. And there isn't a girl on Balfray would walk down this cliff on a dark night at this time of the year. Or any other time of year.'

She paused to let the words sink in and then added, 'The very day Mrs Bliss was drowned, in broad daylight, Letty, who is Saul's cousin and was maid at the castle, was going out to meet her young man's boat coming across from Kirkwall. And she saw, or so she claimed,' she said with a sidelong glance at his mocking expression, 'a seal leap up from the water and drag poor Mrs Bliss under . . . '

Faro stopped walking. 'Is that so? I understood no one witnessed the accident.'

'No one would believe her, being Troller's cousin and always a bit, well, highly strung.'

'Highly strung, indeed. The girl might have been witness to a murder.'

Inga laughed. 'Murder? By a seal man? You can't possibly believe that. Jeremy Faro, after all these years in Edinburgh, I'm surprised at you.'

Faro ignored the taunt. 'And I'm surprised that no one has mentioned this before, Inga. That it was kept so very quiet.' He looked at her. 'Even by you. When you told me how you discovered her.'

Inga shrugged. 'I didn't want to be laughed at,' she said uncomfortably.

'Laughed at, indeed. I think I had better have a talk to this . . . Letty, did you say?'

Inga shook her head. 'She left Balfray just after the accident. Terrified to stay any longer, according to Saul, so she went to Kirkwall and married her fisherman.'

'How can I get in touch with her?'

'Oh, Saul will have her address if you want it.'

'I most certainly do – and soon.'

Inga regarded him steadily. 'You're wasting your time, you know. Letty is only one stage brighter than poor Troller. Alas, it runs in Saul's family. Too many cousins intermarrying.'

'That was one good reason for you not marrying him.' Faro smiled. 'Aren't you glad now that you didn't?'

Ignoring the question, Inga said, 'Fortunately my side of the family didn't inherit madness, only the second sight.'

Faro was silent. 'You should have married, Inga.'

'What makes you say that?' she asked sharply.

'On the evidence of the house we've just left, you would have made a good wife.'

She stopped in her tracks. 'Aren't you a little late with that observation, Jeremy Faro? About twenty years too late,' she added bitterly.

'I'm sorry.'

'Oh, don't be sorry. I've had enough regrets for both of us. Especially when I see Vince. Do you realise we could have had a son about his age?' she added softly, watching his face intently. 'A pity you never had a son of your own.'

'But I did. For a whole week. And then I lost him . . . and my wife too . . . '

She took hold of his arm. 'Oh Jeremy . . . I'm sorry . . . I'm so sorry.'

'You can never be as sorry as I am,' he said harshly. 'As for Vince, he is like my own son, the only one I am ever likely to have.'

His deep sigh, his look of anguish told her how much

he still suffered. 'And now, please, may we change the subject? Aren't we getting a little too personal?'

She returned his smile. 'Just about ready to quarrel. Just as we used to. But there'd be no reconciliation this time, would there?'

Determined to be immune to that soft whisper, the wistful pleading, he replied shortly, 'And no quarrel either, if I can help it.'

They walked in silence and then he asked, 'How well did you know Thora?'

Inga thought for a moment. When she replied Faro detected a certain diffidence, as if she was holding something back.

'Until she took ill, I didn't know her particularly well. I knew Norma much better.' Her tone also indicated that she liked Norma better and Faro, encouraged, asked, 'Tell me about Norma.'

'Oh, I suppose I was sorry for her, having Francis stolen from her by her rich young stepsister. Everyone guessed that Francis was weak and had married Thora for her money. You're not to take anything sinister from that, Jeremy. Women are always sorry for older sisters who are jilted more or less at the altar steps.'

'Norma seemed to have forgiven her, by all accounts.'

She looked at him sharply. 'Yes. Remarkable, wasn't it? Once Thora took ill, Norma couldn't do enough for her. Wore herself to a shadow sitting with her night and day when she had bad turns. Poor Thora, how she did suffer towards the end. Not an ounce of strength and so terribly sick all the time.'

'Did you ever think that her illness was unnatural?'

'Unnatural? I'm not sure I know what you mean by that.'

'Let me put it another way. Did you ever suspect that she might have been poisoned?'

Inga stopped in her tracks. 'Jeremy Faro. You're

impossible, really you are. Stop being so suspicious. Forget you're a detective for once and for heaven's sake act like a normal human being. People in Balfray don't go round poisoning each other.'

'It has been known for husbands to poison wives and vice versa. In my profession it's fairly commonplace.'

'Well, let me tell you, there's nothing of your commonplace here. Everyone loved Thora. Fancy even thinking such a thing about poor Francis. You just have to look at the poor man. It breaks my heart to think of all he has suffered. I've never heard anything so . . . so dreadful . . .'

Stamping her foot indignantly, her colour suddenly high, she gave an exclamation of indignation and turned on her heel.

Faro seized her arm. 'Whoa, Inga. Whoa. I didn't mean to offend you. It's just that the symptoms sound awfully like arsenic poison.'

'Well, they can't be, or Vince wouldn't have signed the death certificate,' she said defiantly. 'There's your answer, plain and straight.'

She stopped and looked down at his hand, still holding her arm. Suddenly she smiled and raising her free hand stroked his fingers in a gentle tender gesture.

'Jeremy, Jeremy,' she said softly, looking up at him. Her touch was no more than the supplication one would give an unruly child but it jolted him. After all those years there was something alarmingly intimate about this contact, this innocent gesture, and it was like a charge of electric current through his veins.

'Inga, Inga,' he said in gentle mockery and firmly released her arm, placing it at her side. The gesture cost him dear, for at that moment he experienced an almost uncontrollable urge to return to a past more than twenty years dead. What would it be like to take her into his arms and hold her trembling to his own wildly beating heart?

That impulse, however, which might have considerably changed his future, was halted by a shout and a wave from the boat which was approaching the landing stage.

A moment later two small figures leaped ashore. Rose and Emily. And behind them trailed Vince.

Chapter Eleven

Faro's first reaction was that he failed to recognise his own daughters instantly. Each time he saw them they looked different from the image he carried in Edinburgh. Guiltily he was aware how quickly children grow and how many changes can take place in a few months.

He was delighted to see them and in the next moment angry that he had not been warned of their imminent arrival, which he would certainly have forbidden, appalled that they should have come to Balfray while he was investigating two, and possibly three, mysterious deaths.

What of the dangers that lurked on the island until the murders of Thora and Troller Jack, for such they undoubtedly were, could be solved? And, as always, the detective was the prime candidate for a cornered assassin's further violence and his family, if accessible, targets for immediate and savage retribution.

'Papa, Papa.' Kneeling, he clasped them both in his arms.

'This is a surprise. I wasn't expecting to see you.'

'But we always come to see Grandma at weekends,' said Rose.

'Now that school has started again,' added Emily.

A quick kiss and they wriggled free to throw themselves into Inga's waiting arms, thrusting the posies they carried at her, hugging and kissing her, while she laughed, breathless and delighted by this onslaught.

She was their friend. Faro listened as they whispered, 'Guess what, Inga? We've been dying to tell you all week . . .'

The world-shattering confidences were only about school and lessons and classmates. Occasionally they glanced in Papa's direction with a shy smile as if they would like to include him. But Papa would not understand. This tall grave man, who sent them gifts but rarely came to see them, was a stranger.

Their shyness made him unaccountably angry and resentful. Vince misinterpreted his expression and murmured apologetically, 'Aunty usually puts them on the boat on Friday, but they were invited to a birthday party last night.'

'Damn,' said Faro, not quite sure who he was cursing at that moment.

Over their heads Inga smiled at him and, firmly detaching the two little girls, said, 'Go and talk to Papa. He's waiting to hear all your news too.'

Faro sensed a slight shuffling of feet as they approached and lined up before him, studying his face intently, unsmiling. They walked towards the castle, carefully holding their father's hands, deferential strangers giving him their doleful, dutiful attention but with many backward glances in Inga's direction. He felt cut to the heart at this reception, jealous and indignant with Inga because they preferred her.

Having successfully stolen his children's affection and loyalty to their father, she walked a short distance away from them. But, turning towards her, he thought he saw something fleeting and forlorn in her expression. It made him suddenly ashamed of his uncharitable emotions.

'Come and join us,' he said.

'There isn't room for us all on the path.'

'Oh there is, Inga,' wailed Rose. 'Plenty of room.'

'Please,' said Faro. 'I want a word with Vince.'

He noticed how they needed no second bidding, clinging to her arm as they raced ahead, laughing, their voices ringing back to him, bell-like with shrill excitement.

Vince mistook his solemn expression. 'Don't worry about them, Stepfather. They'll be all right. No one at Balfray would harm a child.'

'No one but a murderer who might not share your finer feelings, Vince. Well, did you see the Fiscal?'

'Alas, no. He had to go north for an inquiry only yesterday, and, communication between the islands being what it is, he isn't expected back before Monday.'

'Monday,' said Faro in exasperation. 'Hasn't he an assistant?'

'Yes, but he's away to a wedding in Glasgow.' Vince grinned. 'I was told that I had come at a bad time for accidents, they aren't usually as busy as this.'

'What about the newspapers?'

Vince shook his head. 'No luck there, I'm afraid. They only keep one copy of old papers on file which they're reluctant to let out of the office. You'll have to go in and consult them yourself, I'm afraid.'

'Damn!'

'Why not take the girls back to Kirkwall on Monday morning? You could do it then. Any developments to report?'

Faro told him of his meeting with Saul Hoy. 'He doesn't believe in the necrophilia theory. Everyone, according to him and to Inga, thinks the world of everyone else on this island.'

Vince smiled. 'I know that story. Devoted to Troller, while Thora didn't have an enemy in the world. Grandma will tell you the same thing. It could never occur to any of them that Thora had been poisoned and Troller hit over the head with a spade. It's all sweetness and light here. And you don't believe a word of it?'

Faro nodded. 'Not one word, Vince. There's a cesspool of human emotions underneath it all. Someone's lying. That same someone who has killed twice, and maybe even thrice, if we take Mrs Bliss's unfortunate demise into account.'

His brow darkened with sudden anxiety as he looked towards the happy trio of Inga and his two daughters at the castle door. 'And I suspect the killings might have just begun.'

Mrs Faro was waiting to greet her grandchildren and carried them off to the kitchen, from whence appetising smells of baking were ready to supplement her warm welcome in the material sense, calculated to appeal to children everywhere.

Faro declined one of her nice fresh scones more sharply than was polite.

She looked at him. 'What's wrong, Jeremy? You're looking very sour. Come on, eat something. That'll cheer you up, won't it, Vince?'

Without giving Vince a chance to reply, Faro eyed the scene at the table where the two girls had already forgotten his existence and said, 'I wish you'd consulted me, Mother, before bringing Rose and Emily over.'

Her eyebrows raised. 'Consulted you, dear? Why, I thought it would be a lovely surprise. Your two lovely bairns.'

Her reproach set him shuffling his feet uncomfortably. 'It was . . . it was, of course, but . . . ' He scratched his forehead, torn between the necessity of self-justification which would prove him a devoted father but would scare the wits out of his parent. Even he did not feel strong enough to face her reaction to information that within the shadows of Balfray's much-vaunted sweetness and light, there lurked a murderer.

'With the present situation . . . the bereavements and so forth. There'll be the lad's funeral . . .' he ended lamely.

'Not until next week.'

For once the rather excessive eight days' wake that was traditional on the island was in his favour. At least the Procurator Fiscal should have made his report long before the coffin lid was screwed down.

'Oh, they'll be sad, the little darlings,' said Mrs Faro. 'Troller was always so kind and nice to them. But he's gone to Heaven now – like their poor dear mama. They understand that and they'll be happy for him, knowing he's with Jesus.'

Jeremy Faro shrugged. It was a long time since he had believed in the white-clad harp-playing Heaven of his childhood. Years of man's inhumanity to man, of the close confines of the Edinburgh City Police had killed off his innocent piety.

Now, an indifferent churchgoer he had to confess, the faith that had once been his daily bread was the lip-service to be exhibited by his presence at family funerals, weddings and baptisms. It bore no relation to the love of God that had sustained his mother through bitter years of widowhood.

His reaction to a similar situation had been quite different: instead of being fortified by faith, he now bore the Almighty a grudge, wondering if he would ever forgive Him for taking Lizzie and his newborn son.

'Besides, you needn't worry about them getting in the way. They dote on Inga, she's their willing slave,' Mrs Faro added, thereby heaping coals of fire upon his self-doubts. 'She would make a grand wife for somebody.'

Faro closed his eyes and smiled grimly. His mother was nothing if not predictable and he could have won a substantial bet that those would be her next words.

Mrs Faro was saved from a cutting reply when Norma Balfray entered the kitchen.

'Oh, I'm sorry, I'll come back later.'

'No, please stay.'

'Well,' she said doubtfully, 'I only wanted to talk about food.'

Vince had gone up to his room and Faro decided to linger.

'I do apologise once again for neglecting you, Mr Faro. I have been hoping to have a word with you. Perhaps later?'

Faro was pleased she had seized the initiative. Here was a chance, not to be missed, of gaining additional information about the inmates of Balfray, past and present.

He bowed. 'I'll await you in the garden, Miss Balfray.'

She looked puzzled and he left it to his mother to explain that, regarding all smokers as instruments of the devil, as such they were banned from her kitchen. Mary Faro had been trying for many years, quite unsuccessfully, to prise her only son away from the obnoxious habit that had become a necessity for his often frayed nerves. He did not like also to tell her that pipe smoke, so diabolic to her, was a blessed disguise for the viler smells of death and decay that were his daily lot.

A pipe also helped to clear his head remarkably, so while he waited for more pressing domestic matters to be settled, he sat on a bench in the sheltered courtyard whose worn cobblestones had survived three hundred years.

Light laughter and chatter drifted from within the kitchen and as he relaxed in the still warm sunshine, somewhere close by a robin's song pierced the air with poignant sweetness. Not to woo a mate, nor for humans' pleasure and delight, he knew, but from ancient barbarities old as time. Master Robin was marking out his territory for the cruel winter months ahead, when it would be a duel to the death for any of his kind, kin not excluded, to set beak, wing or claw upon this patch he had marked out as his own.

At the sound of Norma Balfray's quick footsteps he doused the pipe. She saw the action and held out her hand.

'Please, Mr Faro. Not on my account. I have no strong feelings about tobacco. Indeed, I enjoy the fragrance much better than cigars. Francis smokes cigars, you know,' she added – an unnecessary apology.

Faro smiled, pocketed his pipe, and indicated the basket she carried. 'May I?'

She seemed surprised at the offer. 'Oh no. I am just going round to the kitchen garden to collect some vegetables. You might be interested in seeing this part of the castle policies.'

Faro offered to accompany her. As a mere man who ate delicious soups regularly but never questioned where the vegetables originated, how they were planted as seeds and grew to maturity, he doubted that his interest in such a hive of domesticity could be long sustained.

The garden surprised him by its size and the fact that it had been laid out with considerable thought. Every vegetable known to the islands had been included and flourished exceedingly. Even the sheltered walls supported apple and pear trees.

'We are safe from the worst of the autumn gales here. And this,' she pointed to a small enclosure, 'this is Inga's herb garden. Here she makes the potions which are guaranteed to cure all ills. I can't tell you how, with the nearest doctor in Kirkwall before Francis arrived, we all came to rely on dear Inga. It's a gift. She knows everything about medicines. She would have made a marvellous doctor, you know.'

What a sublimely ridiculous notion, thought Faro.

From what Vince had told him, the idea of women doctors was considered preposterous and shocking by those in authority. Apart from a few eccentrics it would never catch on, and was greatly to be discouraged. Only a step above nursing, it was considered a less than respectable profession for gentle ladies.

Curiously enough, he could have imagined Norma in such a role. She looked a tougher version of womankind than he normally encountered in Edinburgh upper-class circles. At first glance she was extremely attractive, even seductive. Closer acquaintance revealed a distinctly mannish quality about her walk. As she matched her steps to his, he observed large hands and feet and a sad lack of those deliciously feminine curves demanded and emphasised by the fashions of the day.

'Have you seen the arbour?' asked Norma.

Faro made a non-committal reply, hardly wanting to explain why Vince had taken him the long way round when he had arrived in Balfray.

Norma led the way. 'It's so pleasant and warm. Shall we sit down here?'

A moment later Faro found himself seated on the same seat where Vince had told him that he suspected Thora Balfray had been poisoned and that her stepsister Norma might well be one of the chief suspects.

He now had a chance to observe her features more closely. Each judged apart was a model of perfection: well-shaped mouth and long straight nose, large expressive grey eyes. But it was as if they had been hastily assembled on her face by a creator in such a hurry to finish the task that the wax had not been quite set and they had slipped out of proper alignment.

But all imperfections were forgotten in that next moment when she laughed. Gone was the polite charming mask he had first encountered and he was taken aback unexpectedly by laughter which was ravishing and invested her countenance with a totally unexpected radiance.

Was it this quality of full-blooded mirth that had once captivated Francis Balfray and now had Reverend Erlandson eager to make her his wife? An attractive, strong and competent wife she would be too and, he did not doubt, blithe in bed and at board.

Anxious not to lose this opportunity of delicately framing his first questions, Faro saw that laughter had faded, a slate wiped clean.

'It was about my stepsister Thora I wished to speak to you.' She hesitated. 'I understand that you are a policeman.'

'A detective inspector, actually.'

'That is even better. Detective Inspector,' she sighed. 'Is that how we address you?'

Faro smiled. 'Inspector will do. Or Mr Faro, if you wish.'

She nodded. 'Perhaps you can help us through this dreadful business of the Fiscal's inquiry with as little upset as possible. Like everyone else who knew him, we find it rather hard to understand why poor Troller took Mrs Balfray out of her coffin and laid her on the Odin Stone. But I think we have all, like yourself,' she added with a sidelong glance, 'come to the obvious conclusion.'

'And what would that be, Miss Balfray?'

'That, to his poor demented mind, the stone had magical powers to bring her back to life, of course. Doubtless the effort of lifting her, combined with his injuries when he stumbled and fell down the cliff face in the dark and climbed up again – a little too much to drink, poor boy. Don't you agree?'

'It's certainly within the bounds of possibility,' said Faro, hoping to sound suitably vague and refraining from adding Saul Hoy's testimony.

'And you will impress that upon the Fiscal?' she said anxiously.

'The Fiscal, Miss Balfray, will come to his own conclusions. That is what he is there for.'

'John said he is only called for accidents or suicides.'

Faro saluted the minister's delicacy in not adding murders to the list as she went on, 'We all know it couldn't be suicide. Troller would never have taken his own life. He loved Thora, everyone did, but he was a regular churchgoer. You can ask John about that . . .'

And Faro found himself listening to protestations which were all becoming rather tiresomely familiar. Statements that were firmly qualified by a considerable amount of 'John says' or 'Francis says'.

Sadly he realised that Norma Balfray had nothing to offer which might throw any new light on his investigations and her sole reason for seeking him out was perfectly obvious. To impress upon him, once again, that Troller's odd behaviour had been for the best possible motives and that there was nothing ignoble or impure intended in his removing her stepsister from her coffin.

Most transparent of all was her desperate anxiety that there should be no scandal connected with the family. The necessity of preserving that proud Balfray image of benevolence against which wicked thoughts and dastardly deeds were unthinkable was uppermost in Norma Balfray's mind as she talked to Inspector Faro.

Into this picture of sweetness and light and universal love all were anxious to portray, Faro recognised that the time was inopportune to hint, however delicately, that Thora had been 'accidentally' poisoned. As for Troller and the death scene staged from *Romeo and Juliet*, apparently no one but his brother had envisaged the nastier implications.

Necrophilia, rarely discussed in polite society but a

fact of life, or death, was frequently encountered by Faro in his daily dealings with the lower echelons of society. He had Vince's assurances that it was often criminals who had a basic mind disorder and were deprived of the normal sexual relations with women who found in necrophilia a somewhat revolting satisfaction for their carnal appetites.

Now, anxious to take his leave of Miss Balfray, he found an unexpected excuse in the appearance of Reverend Erlandson, who suddenly materialised from behind the hedge. Flushed in countenance and agitated in manner, he demanded of his betrothed, rather too sharply for politeness, 'I have been searching for you everywhere, my dear. I hardly expected to find you here,' he added sternly.

Faro was acutely conscious that the accusing glance in his direction held a shaft of hardly hidden jealousy, of man-to-man assessment old as time. He left quickly, chuckling to himself. It was rather endearing to find the minister capable of such worldly emotions.

As he hastened towards the castle, he considered that some time spent with his two daughters would be a refreshing change. His final thought on Norma Balfray was to wonder if it had been Francis who had persuaded her to impress Balfray's virtues on the inspector. Or had it been her own idea?

Merry peals of laughter interrupted his reverie and in the distance, quite oblivious of his presence, were Rose and Emily, dancing through the sea wood, holding on to Inga. He stopped, suddenly not wanting to encounter them, not wanting to be a dull appendage to this scene of girlish merriment. But he found himself smiling. They did make a pretty picture.

Fortunate indeed that Rose and Emily had found such a delightful friend. But he realised that he should have been gladder than he felt. Was it only because Inga's reappearance so unexpectedly in his life, as the devoted companion of his two daughters, nagged at him with the unfinished business of yesterday, reminding him that he should remarry?

His girls needed a mother. Everyone told him so. He thought of how happy it would make his mother, and Mrs Brook his housekeeper at Sheridan Place. He thought of friends and colleagues and what an excellent choice, what an adornment, Inga St Ola would be to his bed and board.

As for Vince, he had a shrewd suspicion that his stepson made no addition to this paean of praise. But whatever motives or reasons he might have for not liking his stepfather's choice of a new wife, he would be clever enough to conceal them at all cost. It would be the end, of course, of their shared and undeniably pleasant bachelor existence.

Suddenly angry with himself, Faro turned on his heel and walked quickly in the opposite direction to where the haar gathered like a shroud about the sunshine and the seals increased their doleful lament.

'I'm not prepared to be influenced in choosing a wife. I'll not take a wife to please anyone – except myself. And I'll marry when I'm good and ready, when I want a wife and not a moment before. As for Inga St Ola, with all her herbal cures, her spells, what would I do with a wife who might have the powers to ill-wish another human being to her death?'

Chapter Twelve

Faro decided to call upon Captain Gibb, pondering on how to make it all seem as casual as possible. By now he guessed that the whisper had gone all around sweetness-and-light Balfray warning them that the formidable Inspector Faro was asking questions about Troller's death.

The house near the rectory was stone-built and had at one time been a watch-tower overlooking the bay. Luck was with him, for even as he considered a plausible excuse, the door opened and Gibb beckoned to him.

'I was looking through my telescope watching the seals and I saw you on the cliff path. I was hoping you would come in and have a chat. I understand from Vince that you are interested in the Balfrays' family history,' said the Captain.

The domain of Captain Gibb was very much of the bachelor variety. It sadly lacked a woman's touch and survival, rather than comfort, were the matters most in mind. A general air of untidiness pervaded everything as if each time the Captain took something down from a shelf he made only a half-hearted attempt to replace it.

Much as Faro deplored his busybody mother he had inherited from her a sense of neatness, and living in perpetual disorder outside the confines of his study was painful for him. Following the Captain up the winding stone staircase into what he called his living quarters, Faro observed through a half-closed door an unmade bed.

Another flight of stairs and Captain Gibb opened a door, announcing, 'This is my den.' No description could have been more apt since books toppled from every shelf and papers gushed out of envelopes on to the floor. Somewhere underneath this mountain of words lay a table where, presumably, the Captain sorted through documents concerning the Balfray family. He seemed oblivious to the untidiness. Sweeping aside in one gesture a large heap of rolled documents, he offered Faro a seat, regarding him eagerly from behind a paper hill.

'What can I tell you?' he asked.

This was a poser since Faro hadn't the least idea what Vince had imparted to the Captain. 'Just their history generally. I believe you've found some interesting documents?'

'Indeed, I have. Yes, indeed.' Burrowing for a moment, he at length brought out a tattered notebook. 'I expect you know of their connection with the Earl of Bothwell, Queen Mary's third husband?'

'I have heard some mention of it.'

The Captain nodded delightedly. 'But we go back much, much further than that. There has always been the suggestion of myth and legend about this island. There are certain curiosities, for instance.

'Have you ever considered why there should be trees and vegetation on Balfray when most of the islands have so little?' he added dramatically. 'Has it really something to do with an advantageously sheltered position, or, as legend would have us believe, because it was blessed by St Ola?'

'The saint himself?'

'Yes, a hermit with divine vision, a kind of eleventh-century St Francis. Birds and animals flocked to him and trees grew miraculously to give them shelter. The seals in particular have always haunted Balfray.'

'So I've noticed.'

'Oh dear, I suspect they are rather too noisy at this time of year, St Ola's Summer, that's what it's always been called. The time when, despite what the calendar says, nature forgets it should be preparing for winter and drifts back into summer for a week or two.'

'I'm very glad I timed my visit so well. Orkney, as I remember, at this time of year is plagued with high winds.'

'The rest of Orkney,' Gibb corrected him, frowning at this interruption. 'That is so.'

'I beg your pardon, you were telling me about the saint.'

The Captain shook his head. 'Obviously there had been people living here before St Ola came. The Dwarfie Ha' belongs to pagan days. Have you see it yet?'

'I was much impressed.'

'Good. Good.'

'I presume the Odin Stone is of the same period?'

'Yes, indeed. I'll come to that later,' said the Captain hastily. 'The island was called St Ola, after the saint. It was the Balfrays who changed its name. There is a big gap in the history until St Ola is referred to again in documents dated about 1567 . . .'

'1567? When the Earl of Bothwell was on the run after the Battle of Carberry Hill?'

Gibb chuckled delightedly. 'I see you know your history, Mr Faro. At that time, St Ola was referred to as a place of magic powers which was capable of vanishing into thin air and reappearing every few decades.'

'Eynhallow has a similar reputation.'

Gibb nodded. 'Indeed, indeed it has. Around the time of the Stuart Earls, the island had a reputation which kept sailors and the Earls' men at a respectful distance. Its thick woods and trees were reputed to be the home of a warlock and his sister. No one knows what their names were rightly but they were known to history as the first St Olas.'

Pausing, as if to allow Faro to absorb the significance of this fact, he continued. 'One man wasn't afraid of their reputation. The Earl of Bothwell. Perhaps his own background did not bear too close a scrutiny. He was on the run to put it bluntly and when his ships were refused anchorage they took refuge behind a mist which obligingly hid them from the Kirkwall Castle guns – in this very bay.

'The Earl sought, and found, refuge for several days, made welcome as the guest of the warlock of St Ola and his sister, and waited upon by a strange assortment of creatures, trolls and hogbens, enough to strike terror into human hearts. His compensation was that the warlock's sister was possessed of extraordinary charms, to which the Earl had a known weakness.

'When he took his leave of them, he persuaded the warlock to accompany him on his voyage, a kind of good luck charm, I suppose. He left as payment for Inga St Ola's bed— '

'Inga?'

Gibb nodded. 'Inga St Ola – an extraordinary coincidence, don't you think? Where was I? Oh yes, he left her from his treasures two magnificent emeralds and a chaplet of precious stones – no doubt booty from some of his Border raids, the treasure he was now using as his ransom for his wife, the Queen of Scots. Well, as we know, imprisonment and death awaited him in Denmark, but the warlock escaped, returned to St Ola and built the original castle.

'Rumour had it that Inga St Ola bore Bothwell a child and, with her brother, founded the Balfray dynasty on the booty he'd managed to salvage from the Earl's treasure ship.'

Smiling, the Captain sat back in his chair. 'It's all here in the papers Francis' grandfather found in a leatherbound chest of great antiquity, when he was tearing down the original castle to build the present one. The warlock was a very shrewd man. Magic did not blind him to the practicalities of life on the island. He found a use for everything— '

'Even to using the chambered cairn as the Balfray vault?'

'Clever of you to spot that, Mr Faro. Not quite Maes Howe, but very interesting.'

'What became of the treasure?'

Gibb's eyes gleamed. 'Wouldn't we all like to know that? Most of it vanished into stones and bricks and lost speculations by the family over the years. The Balfray emeralds are all that remains.'

'The ones that Bothwell gave to Inga St Ola?'

Gibb nodded. 'The very same. The family would never part with them. There was a legend that the line would die out if they did. That's here, too, in the papers, if you would like to read it.'

Faro took one look at the cramped ancient writing and winced. 'That's not my interest, alas.'

'Nor mine,' said Gibb cheerfully.

'But how . . . ?'

'Oh, I do know old Scots, but not Latin. I have Reverend Erlandson to thank for translating for me. I desperately needed the help of a scholar. John has been an enormous help, quite tireless. I could never have managed that without him.

'I'm just an old sea-dog,' he added, with a sudden disconcerting roar of laughter, digging Faro in the ribs. 'Am I not, eh?'

Without awaiting an answer, he opened a drawer and

after a deal of searching produced a crumpled parchment and a paper. 'Here's one of John's translations.

> The wicked Earl, the wicked Earl,
> Naen rich as he shall Bee
> 'Til Odin's stayn and Ola's laird
> Doun tae the sea Bee fall.

It still doesn't make a great deal of sense, does it?' Gibb asked with a chuckle. 'As you'll observe on the original, in the place of a word that was missing there was this symbol.'

He pointed to the tiny drawing of a bee and it was a moment before Faro remembered where he had seen a carving exactly like it.

'Remarkable,' he said, handing back the paper. 'And have you ever seen the emeralds?'

Gibb laughed. 'Of course. Everyone has. Thora wears them . . . ' He shook his head sadly. 'I mean, she wore them constantly. Earrings as big as pigeons' eggs, set with diamonds. Beautiful, and these days I reckon still worth a queen's ransom.'

Faro took his departure and returned to the castle, deep in thought. Approaching by the kitchen door he decided that the time had come for a good old gossip with his mother who prided herself on knowing everything.

He was not unduly surprised to see Rose and Emily at the kitchen table, heads poised over the book that Inga was reading to them. As he stood at the door unobserved, it was a cosy domestic scene, the kind he realised that many fortunate husbands experience and take for granted most of their lives, part of their daily homecoming. A sigh escaped him, for he was never to be a husband again, despite that sudden knowing look his mother sent in his direction.

This time the girls leaped up and fluttered to his side with cries of delight. Was it instinctive? was his immediate reaction. Were they glad to see him or was this in response to Grandma's stern lecture on dutiful children?

Smiling, Inga did not linger. She left on some slight excuse and, with Rose and Emily sitting on his knees, a far from comfortable arrangement but one that he was prepared to endure without protest, he tried discreetly to question his mother on events at Balfray Castle.

But mere mention of Thora brought a shake of the head and a frown in the direction of the two girls. Surely this must be one of the oddest police investigations on record, he thought cynically, thankful that Superintendent McIntosh could not see him now.

'Captain Gibb was telling me about the magnificent Balfray emeralds . . . '

'He's always on about something. History is coming out of that man's ears. Can't get any other conversation out of him . . . '

'Did you ever see the earrings?'

'We did, Papa,' said Rose. 'And put them on.'

'Yes, Papa, Mrs Balfray let us wear them,' said Emily proudly.

Faro realised that the two girls, obediently seen and not heard as was required of them, were not completely indifferent to the grown-ups' conversation.

'I would love some earrings,' said Rose. 'Wouldn't you, Emily?'

'Can we have our ears pierced, Papa? Grandma says it doesn't hurt.'

Faro's placating murmur was immediately taken as assent.

'Mrs Balfray took her earrings off when we came to see her.'

'She let us play with them, Papa.'

Faro suppressed a tender smile at this gross exaggeration and the picture of two little girls 'playing' with jewels worth what Captain Gibb had called a queen's ransom.

'Yes, they were so lovely,' sighed Rose.

'Like pigeons' eggs, Papa,' said Emily, with astonishing accuracy, Faro thought, remembering the Captain's description.

'And Mrs Balfray said that maybe some day she would give them to us.'

Mrs Faro exchanged an amused glance with her son. 'I don't think she meant quite that, dear.'

'Yes, she did. Didn't she, Em?'

'One pair of earrings, however valuable, wouldn't be much use between two little girls. And I doubt that you'd want to share them.'

'Mrs Balfray knew that, Grandma. She said we could wear one each, like a pendant.'

Mrs Faro sighed. 'She was very proud of them, the poor love. Her only treasures.' And to Faro, 'She was very fond of these two little lasses of ours.'

'Will we get them now that she's gone to Heaven to be with Jesus?' piped up Emily, shocking her grandmother with this undue display of avarice.

'Yes, Grandma. She did promise,' said Rose.

'Grown-ups often promise things when they are very ill, like Mrs Balfray was,' said Faro, feeling it was time he stepped into the fray, the morals of which had got a little beyond his mother.

'They don't mean to break their promises,' he continued hastily, 'but they aren't always able to keep them. In families when someone dies there are other people who have first claim on jewels and so forth. Do you understand?'

Rose gave a disappointed shrug and as she and Emily

returned to their paints, he said to his mother, 'I would very much like to see these emeralds.'

'I expect Dr Francis would show them to you. Shall I ask him?'

'Not at the moment,' he said hastily. 'Before I leave, perhaps it could be mentioned.'

'Oh, I'll mention it. You know how tactful I can be, Jeremy.'

Faro suppressed a smile as she added, 'It would sound better coming from me than from a perfect stranger.' And, setting the kettle to boil, said, 'What else was Captain Gibb telling you?'

'Just Balfray history.'

'All that stuff about the original St Olas, was it? Do you know what I think?'

Expecting some profound observation, Faro shook his head.

'I think— ' she lowered her voice so that the children would not hear and whispered ' —I think he dyes his hair.'

'That's very observant of you, Mother.'

Mrs Faro gave a nod of satisfaction. 'Funny thing for a respectable gentleman, don't you think?'

'Just human vanity. Men in public office often do it very discreetly.'

'Do they really? But for a Navy man,' she added, 'it just doesn't seem right somehow. Now if he'd been an actor or such like, that would be different.'

A sudden chilling thought jolted Faro. 'How long has he been with the Balfrays?'

'Six months or so, on and off, when he isn't in Glasgow or elsewhere, consulting old records. You'll gather there's not a lot of factoring done by him at the best of times. That was just his excuse to sponge off poor Dr Francis.'

'Is he married?'

'Not him. At least he never mentions a wife or family,' she added with a sniff – of disapproval, thought Faro. Any man who chose bachelordom was a 'queer fish' in his mother's simple maxim of life and how it should be lived.

'Inga told me he was rather sweet on Mrs Bliss – you know, the housekeeper who drowned. Can you credit that?'

Faro smiled and she continued, 'I expect it was because they both arrived on the island about the same time and being strangers that threw them together.'

Faro remembered how mistaken he had been with his idea of a housekeeper in the mould of his mother or the comfortable homely Mrs Brook at Sheridan Place, both long-time widows of an uncertain age. 'By all accounts, it isn't all that surprising that Mrs Bliss appealed to the lonely old bachelor.'

Mrs Faro regarded him, hands on hips. 'Well, it would, it would indeed, if you'd ever seen her.'

He decided to tease her. 'Why, was she an old witch?'

'Not her. She wasn't much past thirty and very bonny, quite an eyeful, I'm told. The Captain was old enough to be her father. It was all very tragic.'

'You think she might have married him if things hadn't worked out so badly?'

Mrs Faro looked across at Rose and Emily and lowered her voice. 'I doubt it. She also had her eye on the minister. Can you beat that? Hers was poor Reverend Erlandson's first funeral on the island, and he was terribly upset.'

And, darting another glance in the children's direction, she whispered, 'Death comes in threes, that's always the way of it. Inga will tell you all about Mrs Bliss, if you're curious.'

Faro was indeed curious as he returned to his bedroom and took out his unfinished notes on the three deaths on Balfray, island of sweetness and light. Three deaths in less than six months.

He was less than ever convinced that Mrs Bliss's death had been an accident. Especially after Inga's revelations regarding the maid Letty who claimed to have seen a seal man drown the unfortunate housekeeper. He didn't believe in seal men, but he did not doubt that a man swimming among seals with wet hair plastered to his head could be mistaken for one of them.

As for Captain Gibb, was his arrival around the same time as Mrs Bliss as coincidental as it looked? Poring over ancient documents when one didn't understand the Latin seemed an unlikely occupation for an old sea-dog vain enough to dye his hair. A genuine historian, or did he have an accomplice on Balfray after bigger game than family papers?

Faro decided it would be worth his while to find out a great deal more about the background of Captain Gibb. His main preoccupation, however, was to have a sight of those priceless emeralds, big as pigeons' eggs. Strange that no one had mentioned them so far, especially as they had been in constant use even during Thora's long illness.

Of more vital importance, where precisely were they now? He hardly thought that such treasures would have been overlooked and forgotten in the ritual of bereavement. But they might well have provided an excellent motive for murder.

He wondered how much Inga knew about the emeralds and, meeting her walking along the tiny beach an hour later, he strongly suspected that she had been following him.

Chapter Thirteen

As they sat on a rock together in the warm sunshine, Faro felt the meeting with Inga, even if somewhat contrived, was also fortuitous. He had little difficulty in leading the conversation to Mrs Bliss.

'Mother tells me that she was very popular with the men.'

Inga laughed. 'True. Captain Gibb was quite besotted and even Saul, I suspect. As for me, it was a pleasant change not to be the object of the island gossips' attention for a while.' She laughed. 'Even John Erlandson used to take long walks with her, although I expect his interest was for the good of her soul,' she added. 'At that time, of course, he hadn't become enamoured of Norma.'

'Ministers are just ordinary men after all, Inga, with the same thoughts and desires,' said Faro. 'It is we who put them on pedestals.'

As he spoke, Inga made patterns with the toe of her shoe in the hard sand. 'They were happy days at Balfray before Thora took ill. The dark cloud of sadness seemed to begin with Mrs Bliss's death.' She sighed. 'As your mother would say, "Death comes in threes." '

Faro smiled. 'That depends on when you start counting. Let's walk, shall we?' He forbore to tell her that there was a quite logical explanation and that, as death was not an infrequent visitor in most large families, one could almost certainly count on another two.

'What happened to all Mrs Bliss's personal effects?'

Inga frowned. 'She had remarkably few. John has plenty of needy people among his parishioners so that disposed of her clothes and so forth. I just remembered, I gave him the tin box with her references and so forth, in case anyone came forward to claim them. All except the notebook your mother found when she was spring-cleaning.'

As they reached the blacksmith's forge she paused with her hand on the gate. 'Can I offer you a cup of tea?'

'I was hoping you would.'

'You know me well enough to ask.'

He followed her into the pretty kitchen where she produced a small red leatherbound book from a drawer. 'In case I forget once again.'

Stirring the fire into glowing embers, she set the kettle to boil and busied herself with the business of buttering scones and setting a couple of tea trays.

To Faro's puzzled 'Four of us?' she replied, 'You're forgetting Troller's wake?' And, nodding towards the upstairs ceiling, explained, 'There are two young people up there keeping vigil. And they will do so day and night until the funeral next week.'

'How very melancholy when they could be outside enjoying the sunshine.'

Inga looked surprised. 'That has always been the custom on Balfray. They come in pairs and many a courting couple enjoy the chance of a little time together. They aren't dismal at all, I can assure you. They sing, play cards, and the girls can be very industrious, they even do a little spinning or knitting.'

She declined his offer to carry the tray upstairs. 'I can manage fine. Unless you wish to pay your respects to Troller.'

He declined and returned to his perusal of Mrs Bliss's

notebook which contained measures that indeed suggested recipes, some vague addresses, and what could only be notes, or reminders, about various Balfray residents. The picture that emerged was of an efficient housekeeper and a methodical woman. But there was nothing beyond domesticity until he turned to the end of the book and found a series of names in bold capitals, BON ESSE BILL BLESS GILES LE BON LEON BLISS.

A code perhaps? And Faro was conscious of a prickling sensation at the back of his neck. Aware of Inga watching him, he asked, 'Have you any idea what this means?'

She looked over his shoulder, frowning. 'A code of some sort. Probably a game she was playing.'

As Faro was about to tear out the page, she said reproachfully, 'Please don't mutilate the book, Jeremy. I don't suppose it's important, but perhaps this should go to John as well.'

'I'm on my way to see him. I'll tell him you want to give it to him,' he added with a smile.

'Here . . . ' she said, producing paper and pen. 'Copy it, if you wish.' She watched him, smiling faintly.

'What is amusing you?' he asked.

'Just the policeman. You cannot bear to be baffled, even by a few meaningless letters in an old notebook. You have to know every mortal thing. Nothing, however unimportant, must be allowed to escape the attention of Detective Inspector Faro.'

He could think of no suitable reply to that.

Next morning, he awoke to the sound of church bells and for a moment thought he was back in Sheridan Place, but it was Mrs Faro and not Mrs Brook who carried in the breakfast tray.

Opening the curtains, she said, 'Look sharp, Jeremy. Or we'll be late for church.'

'Church?' he demanded weakly.

'What else on a Sunday morning?' was the reproachful reply.

Faro lay back with a groan. He could have thought of several other things that particular morning, for his sleep had been disturbed and restless, plagued by strange visions and vivid dreams, the consequence of a gale force wind rattling the windows. At such times living on an island felt somewhat insecure.

'Vince is already up and about, has been for hours.' His mother sighed. 'He's been attending to poor Dr Francis.'

'Is he ill?'

'He's been ill for weeks now, but no one has had time for his sufferings. I've been telling them, ever since poor Mrs Balfray died . . . He took a bad turn in the middle of the night.'

'What kind of a bad turn?'

'His heart, I think.'

'In that case, perhaps I'd better stay.'

'What good would you do here? You're a policeman, not a doctor. Besides, Rose and Emily will be so disappointed if, on the rare occasions you see them, you don't accompany them to church. They so look forward to a family occasion and it sets them a good example.'

Half an hour later the entire Faro family made its way across the stormy headland to Erlandson's church. To his stepfather's anxious question about Francis, Vince replied, 'I've made him as comfortable as I can.' And, seeing Mrs Faro listening eagerly, he said, 'Nothing too serious.' But the pressure on Faro's arm indicated that there would be more related on that subject later.

The Episcopal Church was a severe shock to Jeremy Faro, reared in the strict Calvinist doctrine of the Reformation. There was more than a sniff of popery, he thought, about Balfray's church, with its incense, the congregation's responses and genuflections. He soon lost his place in the order of service. But his mother, who had adapted with creditable speed from her staunch Church of Scotland roots, took great pleasure in pushing him in the right direction and whispering that it would all be over in less than an hour.

He was interested to see Reverend Erlandson in his elaborate priestly robes; surprised, too, at the inspired oratory of this normally quiet unassuming man who so rarely appeared in the uniform of his calling.

The pulpit indeed endowed him with a new authority and his passionate delivery reverberated through the church, emphasising Faro's first impression of an Old Testament prophet from a medieval tapestry. As Balfray chaplain, John Erlandson also seemed to have a free hand in the matter of family worship.

As Mrs Faro had suggested the fashionably lengthy sermon was omitted and Faro sat back as comfortably as the hard pew would allow to enjoy and absorb this relatively new experience and let that splendid voice pour over him. A moment later, Erlandson's text from the Epistle of Paul to the Romans jolted him into immediate attention.

' "Recompense to no man evil for evil. If it be possible live peaceably with all men. Have more than thou showest, Speak less than thou knowest, Lend less than thou owest." Paul goes further, dear friends, he continues, "Consider man well. He owest the worm no silk, the beast no hide, the sheep no wool, the cat no perfume. Therefore, I beseech you, owe no man anything, but to love one another." Amen.'

As Reverend Erlandson solemnly closed his Bible and invited worshippers to join in the closing hymn, Vince observed a familiar air of excitement about his stepfather, an almost gleeful elation as they left the church. Vince sighed. Short as the service had been, he had found it somewhat trying, his main concern being to return to the bedside of Francis Balfray.

Greeting Erlandson in his handsome robes, shaking hands with his little flock, as he called them, a proud and doting Norma Balfray hovering at his side, Vince murmured to Faro, 'It would seem that the minister has a less active role in the Episcopal Church.'

'So you noticed that too?'

'Yes, one just needs to follow the order of service slavishly, that's all. Not much room for originality, or much work in preparing sermons, I should have thought.'

Faro didn't answer and Vince, walking between his two stepsisters who proudly clung to his hands, gave his stepfather a curious look. 'You seemed to enjoy it all, despite your reluctance. At least the sermon was gratifyingly short.'

'Short, yes. But an odd choice, don't you think?' was the reply.

'Indeed? Tell me, what was wrong with it?'

It was Vince's turn to be intrigued but there was little chance of discussing the sermon as Inga St Ola was welcomed into the family group.

Faro found that once again he was forgotten by his daughters. He was not alone this time. Their beloved stepbrother Vince was also abandoned and he exchanged a glance of mock despair with Faro as they watched the two little girls who, despite chidings from their grandmother to remember this was the Sabbath, rushed to Inga's side with gleeful cries.

She was looking particularly attractive and elegant, Faro thought, in her Sunday-best shawl with a velvet bonnet capturing the long black hair into a semblance of neat coiffure. The bustle, that rage of Edinburgh, with its tight corseting distorting the female form, had not yet made its appearance in Orkney where women wove their own cloth for homespun simple gowns and shirts for their menfolk. Most of the children wore cut-downs, turned and remade from the adults' outworn or outgrown garments.

Was he becoming used to Inga's place in his family, Faro wondered? Envy and resentment were fast-fleeting, fading. And he did not miss the speculative glances from his mother as he regarded, smiling gently, the pretty trio his daughters made with Inga St Ola.

'Inga usually takes them for a picnic on a Sunday,' said Mrs Faro, 'while I have my afternoon rest. Of course, they won't expect that when their papa is here.'

She was wrong. Even as she spoke, Rose and Emily darted back and seized her hands.

'Can we go with Inga? Please, Grandma.'

'Don't be asking me. Ask your papa.'

Aware of this family stir, Inga came forward and, regarding his unsmiling face, said sternly, 'There won't be any picnic today, not unless your papa comes too.' Then smiling at him she asked softly, 'Will you join us, please, Jeremy?'

Faro frowned, intent on eating his Sunday dinner as fast as his mother would allow and retiring to his room immediately afterwards. There he would spend the afternoon adding his recently acquired information to his notes, and considering some new and very disquieting theories about the Balfray murders.

Now he saw three anxious and very pretty faces regarding him. 'Perhaps I might come along later. How would that be?'

'You do mean it, Papa? Promise.'

'I can't promise, Rose, but I'll do my best.'

'We go to the Troll's Cave, along the shore.'

'We discovered it, didn't we, Em?' said Rose.

'It's our secret,' said Emily. 'But we share it with Inga, 'cause she's special.'

'And Vince and Papa, too, Em. They can come.'

'This Troll's Cave, is it safe?' Faro demanded.

Inga smiled. 'Of course it is, or I wouldn't take them there,' she added reproachfully.

Rose took her hand defensively. 'And we aren't allowed to go there on our own. We promised Inga and Grandma that we wouldn't ever go without a grown-up.'

'There's a fairy wishing pool, Papa,' said Emily temptingly.

Inga put her arm around Rose's shoulders. 'It's a very sheltered spot, even in winter. And they do love it so.'

Faro smiled. 'Very well, I'll try and come later.'

Inga looked pleased. 'Now I must go and give Saul his dinner and pack the picnic basket.'

As she turned to go, Faro murmured in what he hoped was a whisper inaudible to his mother, 'By the way, I'd like another look at Mrs Bliss's notebook, if I may.'

'I thought you had got all the information you needed.' She turned and pointed to the porch where Captain Gibb and the minister were deep in conversation.

'The Captain looked in after you'd gone. He saw the notebook still sitting on the table and he got very agitated. As I told you, he was very upset when Mrs Bliss had her accident. He told me he had given her the notebook and seeing it there brought it all back again. He was quite tearful.'

She shrugged. 'I let him have it, and he said he would hand it to John to put with her other possessions. I rather think he'll keep it, though, a sad memento, poor man.'

'Come along, Inga. 'Bye, Papa.'

''Bye, Vince.'

Faro looked across at his two daughters standing in the kirkyard, their hands raised in farewell, their bonnet ribbons fluttering in the sea breeze. Time had suddenly stood still and they had become lifeless portraits painted in a medieval age. The sight made him shiver.

Without them, I am nothing. I am a dead man.

With the feeling of death's angels fluttering near, he was suddenly overwhelmed by his love for them, his yearning to rush over, take them in his arms and protect their gentle trusting innocence against all the world's dangers and evils.

Danger. That was it. That was why the feeling was so familiar and he knew that it was imperative that he crack this case. He must get away from this island of sweetness and light with its underlying cesspool of corruption and hypocrisy. There was no time to be lost, he knew the urgency of the next few hours. At least his daughters weren't in danger, they would be safe with Inga.

When they reached the castle, Vince followed Faro upstairs, where both men were anxious to change into more comfortable clothes and Faro searched for a shabby tweed outfit, somewhat out of date and once sold in Edinburgh under the misnomer, where Faro was concerned, of 'sports costume for gentlemen'.

'This should be suitable for the picnic.'

'So you've decided to go after all,' said Vince. 'In that case, I'll come with you.'

'I have to make some notes, but with luck I'll be ready to bring you my latest findings on our murderer.'

Vince nodded absently. 'I hope Francis is well enough to be left. I'm very worried about him, and I feel the next few hours might be crucial.'

'Crucial? In what way? I didn't realise he was seriously ill, Vince.'

Vince looked unhappy. 'He isn't. I feel it has more to do with the mind than the body. And that is why

I don't want him to wake up and find himself alone. In his terrible despair, he might . . . well . . . ' With a gloomy shake of his head, he left the sentence unfinished. 'Tell me about your findings, Stepfather. Some new developments?'

'Yes, Vince. On three deaths. And all of them were murders, beginning with Mrs Bliss— ' He was interrupted by the sound of footsteps and Mrs Faro looked round the door.

'Your dinner is ready. Come along.'

'I'll go and take a look at Francis,' said Vince.

'You'll have your dinner first,' said Mrs Faro. 'Dr Francis has just woken up and he is having a glass of warm milk.'

There was no possibility of further discussion with Vince who left the table, as soon as decency would allow, to attend Francis. Meanwhile, Faro retreated to his bedroom where he wrote out a comprehensive report on the three murders on Balfray Island.

By the time he laid aside his pen, he was almost certain who had murdered Mrs Bliss and why Troller had met his untimely end. Only the motive remained obscure and where it connected with Thora Balfray, linking the three murders.

He had decided to put his new theory to Vince when he was distracted by the sound of rain drumming on the window. With the suddenness that characterises weather changes in Orkney, the golden afternoon had vanished into mist.

Sighing, he went downstairs to the kitchen, wondering why it was so quiet. He smiled at the sight of his mother enjoying one of her rare periods of silence. He stood looking down at her, overwhelmed by a rush of love for his so-often exasperating parent. But even his gentle kiss on her forehead did not awaken her.

At that moment he heard Vince on the stairs.

'How is Francis?'

'He's responding well, but I didn't feel that I ought to leave him for the afternoon.' He smiled. 'So you missed the picnic, too, Stepfather?'

'I'm just on my way there now . . . '

The chiming clock behind them struck four.

'Is that the time? It can't be,' said Faro, taking out his watch. With the same thought in mind the two men exchanged glances.

'Shouldn't the girls be back by now?' Faro asked.

'They should have been ages ago, considering the weather.' Vince pointed to the windows. 'It's been pouring down for the past hour. And blowing up a gale too.' He made a helpless gesture. 'Look, I was sitting with Francis, reading. Naturally I presumed you had gone off without me.'

Faro fought rising panic which began somewhere in the region of his heart. 'Inga has probably taken them home with her.'

'With a wake in progress under her roof? I don't think that's very likely— '

'Listen . . . listen . . . ' Even above the wind, they could hear a rhythmic beating, the boom of an angry sea.

Faro gripped Vince's arm. 'The tide's in. That's the high tide.'

He was aware that Vince's face had drained of all colour. 'Dear God . . . you know what that means, Stepfather? The Troll's Cave must be under water . . . '

But Faro hardly heard as he threw open the front door.

Chapter Fourteen

As they raced along the cliff path the sea was already roaring over the rocks, throwing up a boiling fury of spray which, allied to the rain, drenched them.

'Where is this Troll's Cave, anyway?' Faro panted.

'Up there, see that batch of arched rocks . . . near the lighthouse.'

'Dear God . . . it's miles away.'

Vince drew alongside. 'Don't worry, Stepfather,' he gasped. 'I'm sure we're worrying quite unnecessarily . . . Inga will have them sheltering somewhere . . . they'll be perfectly safe . . . '

Faro had no breath left for an answer, saving every ounce of effort for the steep incline. But, before he reached the path where the lighthouse towered above the shore, he knew with a sickening jolt of terror that the cave where his children played was under water and had been for the past hour.

Panic seized him, the ground shaking, the water roaring, the sound of doom, funnelling up the rock chimney, covering him with spray.

'Rose! Emily!'

But their shouts were in vain. The two men exchanged horrified glances for below them everything had ceased to exist and nothing remained but the sea. A grey sea, with billowing white-crested waves. Even the seals had deserted this angry monster, and only the sea-birds screamed above their heads, an endless litany, a mocking requiem for the folly of man's struggle against the elements.

Both men were now incapable of reason. All they could think of was the two children drowned, drifting out to sea, hurled back and broken on the savage rocks below. As men have done since the beginning of time and upon these very shores, many a time and oft, they ran back and forward up and down the path, waving their arms, shouting.

Stopping occasionally to peer out into that deadly implacable enemy, the sea, they were not only beyond reason, but beyond control. Few of their friends would have recognised Vince or Faro in their sodden clothes, in their extremes of grief, their countenances distorted with fear as the tears ran unchecked, spurting from their eyes, blinding them, but brushed aside unheeded.

At last Faro stood still, stared up at what he could discern of where he believed heaven to be, if it existed at all. He threw his arms wide, prepared to make the supreme gesture of renunciation. He would give up everything, everything he possessed. He would walk the world a pauper, never take on another case, he would give his own life gladly, if only God would spare his two bairns.

'Look . . . over there!'

Not a divine answer, but sweet as the word of God, Vince calling again. 'Look, Stepfather, look!'

And above the seabird's lament, a fainter human call.

'Help! . . . Help!'

Through the wild spray, one tiny figure precariously perched on a rock still above the sea, waving, piteously crying.

'Rose! It's Rose!'

Fleeter, faster than his stepfather, Vince was already leaping down the cliff face. But Faro was close at his heels. And, in the time it took to reach his elder daughter, he had already come to terms with the grief fate held in store.

It ill became any father, a widower in particular, to have a favourite child. Rose was nearer to him, so like himself, clever, already showing signs of a keen perceptive mind. The apple of his eye was spared this day, but there was a price and he must pay it in full. To live for the rest of his life with the guilt of remorse for little Emily, his baby, who was lost.

The thunder of that cruel triumphant sea, the scream of the gulls deadened all hope of coherent words. His vision blurred by tears, he held Rose close. His tears mingling with her own, he cursed his own folly, his own arrogance. In God's name why had he considered finding the Balfray murderer more important than his own loved ones' safety? Had he gone out with them this afternoon, instead of devoting himself to notes and deductions, both would still be alive.

Lifting Rose in his arms to carry her to safety, he heard Vince's joyful voice and turned to see him clutching a tiny woebegone figure who had huddled unobserved in a crevice, sheltering against the blast of wind and sea.

'Emily . . . oh my heart's darling, my little Emily.'

And handing Rose to Vince, he took her, held her to his heart with such a cry of 'Thank God, thank God' that even the storm at that moment seemed stilled and held back in awe as one man's cry drifted to the very threshold of eternity.

A few moments later and two still sobbing drenched children were safe on the cliff path.

'Inga. Where's Inga? Why isn't she with you?' Vince demanded.

And, for the first time, Faro realised the enormity of Inga's absence and what it might portend. It took some little time before Rose could answer through her sobs, by which time Faro feared the worst.

'She . . . lost . . . something. As we were going to the cave. She said . . . she would be back in a minute.'

'Are you sure, dear?'

'Yes, Papa. While we were putting out the picnic she said she had to go and look for her watch, but she wouldn't be gone an instant.'

'When was this?'

'I don't know, Papa. Soon after we arrived. The tide hadn't even turned. It was a long way out then, wasn't it, Em?'

Emily tugged at her sister's sleeve. 'Tell Papa, Rose.'

'No, you tell him.'

'When she didn't come back, we were hungry and we ate all the fruit cake,' Emily said shamefacedly. 'Do you think she will be cross, Papa? We left the cheese and bannocks,' she added enthusiastically.

Instead of scolding them, their father laughed delightedly and the girls exchanged glances. Fancy Papa approving of their neglect of good nourishing – and filling – food for forbidden treats.

Hardly able to tear himself away from them, but aware of wet clothes and growing chill, in sight of the castle, he put them firmly in his stepson's care. 'Vince will take you home and Grandma will give you both a nice hot bath and something special for tea.' He added so many instructions about keeping warm, and not catching cold, that Vince's mocking glance told him what he knew already. In matters of anxiety he sounded, even to his own ears, exactly like his mother.

'I'll be back as soon as I can. I'm going to look for Inga.'

Vince nodded. 'I wonder what excuse she'll have to offer.'

'Excuse?'

'Yes, Stepfather, isn't it obvious?' said Vince coldly. 'Leaving the children to go and look for a watch and then failing to come back for them. Quite extraordinary, don't you think?'

Faro felt impelled to say, 'She's so fond of them, I can't imagine her letting them get into any danger. There must have been a very good reason.'

'For leaving your children to drown?' was Vince's indignant reply. 'Can you think of any reason on God's earth to justify such behaviour?'

As Faro hurried off again in the direction of the cliff path, he realised that leaving the children, as Vince had implied, was quite out of keeping with Inga's character.

Unless . . . unless . . . Inga St Ola had a role in the sinister events at Balfray. And what about that tiny boat, bobbing on the tide, now far out to sea and once moored near the shore?

His common sense told him that a desperate woman on the verge of discovery might consider that the loss of the Detective Inspector's two children would dismiss all other urgent matters, such as tracking down a clever murderer, from his mind. In that, of course, she would have been right. And how well she knew him. No one better, he realised grimly.

The first and obvious place to look was at the smithy. Saul Hoy opened the cottage door wearing his Sunday-best clothes. He shook his head, surprised but unalarmed by the question.

'She's not here. She left soon after dinner and told me she was taking the two peedie girls for a picnic down at Troll's Cave. That's what she does every Sunday when they're staying at the castle.'

Pausing, he regarded Faro's expressionless face. 'You must have missed them somehow. Probably taken them home through the sea wood.'

Faro retraced his steps. So where was she? Added now to the anger of her possible betrayal was fear that such speculation was not justified. Inga, he told himself, was not a monster who would leave two children to drown, or he could never have loved her long ago . . .

He stopped, suddenly chilled by a new thought. Could that, in fact, be the reason why she had abandoned Rose and Emily so heartlessly? Because she still loved him and knowing she would never have any children of her own, she wanted to punish him for the past?

It was not beyond the bounds of possibility. He had already witnessed a re-enactment of *Romeo and Juliet*, so perhaps Greek tragedy, too, had a place on this accursed island. Some instinct told him to be more charitable, that there was a more plausible explanation for her desertion, some event over which she had no control.

Afterwards, he wondered why he had never considered that she herself might be in danger, a fact not without significance when it came to assessing his own feelings about her. Had he been in love, he realised, then the possibility of her being in danger would have been his first consideration. He would have been mad with terror, not calm and speculative.

Baffled, calling her name occasionally, he had almost regained the cliff path when he heard a sound from a ditch alongside. Moving aside the weedy hedgerow, he saw Inga lying there. She seemed to be sleeping but when he shook her, she did not move. For a moment he thought that she was dead, then her eyes fluttered open. Sobbing, she clung to him.

'The girls, oh, Jeremy, the girls,' she moaned, and struggled to sit up. 'The tide will be coming in. We must go to them.'

'It's all right, Inga. They're safe.'

Bewildered, she looked around her. 'But the tide . . . what time is it?'

'Five o'clock.'

'Five o'clock,' she screamed and jumped to her feet,

staggering back into his arms with the effort. 'The tide . . . Jeremy. It's past high tide.'

'They're safe, Inga, safe back at the castle. We rescued them. Don't you understand?'

She sank to the ground again. 'Thank God. Thank God you were in time.'

He sat beside her, took her icy hands in his. 'What happened, Inga? Whatever made you leave them?' And he heard his own anger rising now that she was apparently unharmed.

'We'd just reached the cave, when I realised I'd lost my watch, dropped it somewhere on the way down.' She looked at him, appealing, 'It's my most treasured possession, Jeremy, you gave it to me for my twenty-first birthday. Sent it all the way from Edinburgh, don't you remember?'

And, regarding his bewildered stern face, she sighed softly. 'No, I see you don't. You'd forgotten long ago.'

'Go on,' he said, ashamed of his harsh unfeeling tone. A woman's silly sentimental whim about a watch had almost cost his children their lives.

'I knew I must try to find it,' she sighed.

'I see you're wearing it, so your search was successful.'

Touching the watch, caressing it, she nodded. 'I found it near the ditch here, just a few steps away. I was looking to see if it had been damaged, when I heard footsteps running behind me. I turned, thinking it might be you, but – whoever it was – he, or she, wore a cloak. I saw an arm upraised and I knew nothing more until I saw your face looking down at me. That's the truth, Jeremy.'

'You mean . . . you were attacked?'

'Well, I didn't hit myself on the back of the head, I assure you. I have quite a bump . . . ouch. Oh, please don't . . . '

'Let me . . . ' The framed bonnet she was wearing was

certainly slightly dented and had taken the worst of the blow, but when he touched her head, she winced again.

Shaking his hand free she stood up with considerable effort, and took a few unsteady steps. 'I'm all right, Jeremy. Everything is all right as long as the girls are unharmed.'

'Have you any idea who attacked you? Describe him again, if you please.'

She shook her head. 'I didn't get a chance to have a good look at him, did I, whoever it was?'

'Have you ever heard of anyone else being assaulted in a similar way?'

'Of course not,' she said scornfully. 'Balfray folk don't go round viciously attacking each other.'

But her assailant, Faro thought, sounded remarkably like the one Vince had told him about. The cloaked man with a taste for practical jokes Francis had encountered, with almost fatal consequences, on that same narrow cliff path when he was riding home on horseback.

'So you have no idea who it might have been?'

'Not the slightest.' With a sigh, she put her hand to her head. 'All I want to do, if you don't mind and you're finished asking questions, is to get home as quickly as possible. I have a splitting headache.'

'Perhaps you should get Vince to look at it.'

'If it's still sore tomorrow, I will.'

How weary she sounded and suddenly ashamed of his false suspicions and his unchivalrous behaviour, Faro said, 'I'll see you to the door.'

'If you would be so good. I'd be most grateful.'

He offered his arm and she leaned on him gratefully. 'I really do feel rather groggy. I must go and lie down for a while. I promise to answer all your questions later. But I really haven't anything to add to what I've told you already.'

'You will be all right?'

She seemed surprised by the sudden concern in his voice and managed a small uneasy laugh. 'Of course I will.'

He stood at the gate looking at her, wondering what he'd missed, what vital information was being withheld. 'I hope you aren't going to tell me that you haven't an enemy in the world, either,' he said sternly.

'Oh no, Jeremy, you would never catch me saying that.' And smiling mockingly up into his face, she said, 'At almost any given moment, I could present you with an impressive list of people who don't like witches, even white ones – people who would be very glad to avail themselves of an opportunity to hit me over the head on a Sunday afternoon, or any other day of the week, come to that.'

Faro left her thoughtfully. Had the attacker marked down Inga as his fourth victim? If so, what did Inga know and what piece of vital information was she withholding and for what reason?

Or were his two children to be the next victims of a crazed and vicious murderer? He went suddenly cold at the thought. Then anger overtook him, the clear-thinking merciless anger which was relentless in its pursuit of violent criminals who threatened the safety of his own family.

And his feelings were stronger than ever that the answer to all three deaths lay with the first murder – of the housekeeper, Mrs Bliss.

Chapter Fifteen

In the face of the day's happenings, and the sinister unknown elements at work, Faro was not prepared to risk another night with his two precious children under the roof of Balfray Castle.

He made up his mind to leave on the evening tide, taking them back with him to the safety of their Aunty Griz's house in Kirkwall. There, on the following morning, he would set about tracking down, in the offices of *The Orcadian* and the police station, some answers to the question which plagued and baffled him.

He was acutely aware of the difficulties of solving a murder case on a small island, where the word 'urgent' had not yet been invented and communications with the outside world, by telegraph, were non-existent. For the first time, Faro realised how greatly he had come to depend on the organisation of the Edinburgh City Police.

Kirkwall, discernible as a whale-like shape on the horizon when visibility was good, seemed tantalisingly near. Lying twenty minutes away by boat, it might as well have been two hundred miles away. Balfray relied on the mailboat twice per week, or else made the short journey by acquiring a small craft with, mercifully, a boatman skilled in the ways of those treacherous waters.

Mrs Faro was taken aback at her son's rash decision, which she considered was totally irresponsible, especially as his experience of rowing boats and navigating them across dangerous channels was nil. 'But I'll be getting the bairns ready for their bed shortly. Taking them out at this time of night. Can't it wait until morning? A peedie note to the teacher – after such an adventure, she'll surely excuse them coming in late.'

Faro shook his head. 'No, mother. Such an excuse would be a lie. Look at them,' he added, regarding the two girls curled up rosy and warm before the fire, with a tender smile. 'See for yourself. They are none the worse for their experience. Haven't taken a bit of harm.'

Mrs Faro continued to frown and he patted her cheek gently. 'Don't worry about them, dear. They'll enjoy this new adventure. Don't you see?'

Apparently oblivious to the conversation between their elders, Rose looked up briefly. 'Can we really stay up late, Papa, and go sailing with you . . . ?'

'Just like grown-up ladies – at night?' echoed Emily in tones of awe.

'Just this once,' he said, watching them leap to their feet with yells of delight, demanding boots and capes, fussed over by their grandmother.

He could not tell her the truth but he was more frank with Vince who also urged him to wait until Monday morning. Faro waved aside his protests. 'Look, I'm going and that is all there is about it. My scalp prickles and I still sweat with fear when I think what might have happened this afternoon. I can't devote all my powers of deduction to facts in this case that are staring me in the face because I'm so afraid of what harm might come to my children.' He shook his head. 'I want to make sure they are quite safe and that our murderer cannot again make them innocently serve as a weapon against me.'

'Again?' demanded Vince. 'You mean he has done so already?'

'He, or she, Vince,' Faro said solemnly and then

shaking his shoulders he added, 'So I intend to go, even if I have to row the boat across myself.'

Watched anxiously by Vince, he threw some clothes into a bag.

'I should come with you, Stepfather. You're such a rotten sailor. I don't like the idea of you being in charge of a boat.'

'Precisely. If I am in charge, it will be an excellent cure for seasickness, in that I won't have time to think about it.'

'That's all very well, but . . . '

Faro laid a hand on his shoulder. 'But me no buts, lad. Every hour is crucial to our murderer. So one of us must stay and your presence here is needed most, to keep an eye on Francis.'

'I don't know what you'll do, if the weather turns rough.'

But, remaining true to its record of unpredictability, Balfray rounded off its day of storms with a sunset of towering majesty, turning the sea to wine, filling the large windows of the castle and spilling through its rooms the rose-glow of a dying day.

Downstairs Mrs Faro, recognising her son's steely inflexibility, remembered that Annie's young brother was courting a lass in Kirkwall and he had his own boat.

'And he'll be delighted to take you with him, Jeremy,' she said, breathless after running upstairs. 'But you'll need to look sharp.

'And I'll be a lot happier, I can tell you,' she muttered to Vince, watching the trio gather in the hall.

'Me, too, Grandma,' whispered Vince, giving her a hug.

On the doorstep, Faro turned to Vince and said, 'By the way, try not to leave Francis alone more than is absolutely necessary.'

As they set off it seemed that they sailed in a painted boat across a painted sea. Calm as glass, the sunset had been replaced by huge moving curtains of light, with every colour of the kaleidoscope drifting over the sky.

'It's the Merry Dancers, Papa,' said Rose, watching the pale streamers shot with shafts of brilliant colour.

No wonder ancient people had lived in fear of the aurora borealis, Faro thought, imagining that this signalled the end of the world, a prelude marking the descent of angry gods to the earth.

Looking back towards Balfray, the island seemed insubstantial. Swaying between earth and sky it floated, illuminated by the lighthouse's intermittent beam and a full moon which arose carving a path of silver across the water. Above their heads an arch of stars stretched out to eternity.

In answer to his question, yes, they knew the names of the stars, did his clever little daughters. As their far ancestors had once steered their dragon-headed warships from across the sea to the Orkney Isles by the chart of the heavenly bodies, so were these small children still schooled in the ways of planets and distant stars, ways already long forgotten in the lamplit streets of Edinburgh.

Faro fell silent, an arm around each, holding them close, suddenly inordinately proud as they solemnly pointed out Orion the hunter, Sirius the dog, Castor and Pollux the shining twins, and the Seven Sisters.

'And over there in the west, Papa, the very brightest of all, that's Venus, first to rise and last to set.'

The earthbound red stars on the horizon became identifiable as gleams from lamplit windows in Kirkwall. As they stepped ashore on the quayside where sailors and fishermen Sunday-evening walked, Faro listened again to the familiar accent that had once been his own. A lost world of dialect, where harbour sounds and clear air brought back the past with heart-searing clarity and he entered again a world of senses.

Touch, sight, and long-forgotten smells of ships and sea brought back vivid recollections of days buried under the drift of years, reviving their joys and their sorrows. He found himself once more briefly captive in that magic girdle of a childhood where those who died went safely to Heaven.

The wickedness of man belonged to ogres in the story books. Only in fiction could innocent children be left to drown, unwanted wives poisoned and a crazed young man brutally murdered with a spade. In the world he had lost long ago, such evil as he had left in Balfray never happened to you or to the people you loved.

Aunty Griz's cottage was a step away from the quayside and whoever brought the children back to Kirkwall could be relied upon to see them safely to her door, which was never locked. Indeed, if there had ever been a key to it, she had never seen it in her lifetime. She threw down her knitting and looked up in wonder as Faro stepped across the threshold. A moment later she exclaimed in shrill delight and threw her arms about him.

'I was wondering who the big handsome man was. I declare you get better looking with every passing year, lad.'

Hospitality in the form of tea, bannocks and oatcakes was immediately forthcoming, as important in this humblest of abodes as in the laird's castle he had just left.

Rose and Emily rushed to set the table with instructions whirling round their heads and he was touched to find his unexpected visit was a gala day for Aunty Griz.

'No, lambies, one of my nice tablecloths, if you please.'

It was one she had embroidered herself forty years ago for her marriage chest, but no husband had ever come to claim her and she would die, he did not doubt, as she had lived all her life, a virgin.

'Rosie lass, never those old cups, what are you thinking about?' she said with a look of apology in Faro's direction as the offending cups were speedily replaced with the delicate best china. A teaset brought back long ago by her sea captain father from some exotic seaport far from Stromness.

Remembering with shame how irritated he was with his mother's fussing, Faro found himself, at the end of a long and sorely troubled day, very happy to be cosseted and waited upon, sitting in front of a large peat fire and listening to tales of his past.

'I mind it well, even as a peedie lad, you were always that determined, always on the move, always wanting to be somewhere else. Never a bit of patience . . .'

Even to his own ears, they hardly sounded the right attributes for his chosen mission in life where patience, the ability to bide one's time until they made another mistake, was the rule for catching criminals.

And, at the end of an alarming list of his shortcomings, despite the telling with wry humour, Faro was surprised to meet himself as a somewhat disagreeable child. When he said so, Aunty Griz smiled. 'Aye, but you were always that clever and kind, especially to poorer bairns and animals. You were a bairn yourself for a shorter time than most,' she added with a sigh and picked up her knitting again.

'You seemed to have grown-up sense when your mother came back home after your poor dear father died. "I'm going to take care of her, Aunty." That's what you said.' Her laughter crackled. 'And you not yet started the school. So protective and loving. You haven't changed, by all accounts.'

Guiltily aware that it wasn't true and that he, for long periods, neglected his mother and bairns, he said lightly, 'It must run in the family, Aunty Griz. We must get it from you for you've been so good to all of us.'

She looked across at Rose and Emily and nodded. 'They're fine bairns you have, fine bairns, Jeremy Faro. You must be proud of them.'

Faro chuckled. 'Thank God, Rose and Emily take after their mother.'

'Aye, poor Lizzie. I only met her the once, ten years ago, was it? You were on your honeymoon and Rose not even thought of.' She shook her head. 'I could see yon was a very special lass. Right for you.'

As the silence threatened to throw them into sorrowful remembrance, Aunty Griz laid aside her knitting and said briskly, 'It's time those bairns were getting to bed, Jeremy. It won't be like this in the morning, I can tell you. Long faces, cross tempers too – the trolls will have taken away the little angels you see tonight and replaced them with their own nasty-tempered bairns.'

'We'll go, Aunty Griz, if Papa will read to us,' said Rose sweetly.

'Now there's a good girl. Your bed's warmed and there's been a fire lit since teatime.'

From the white depths of the great bed where she and Emily slept, Rose handed him *Tales from Shakespeare*, one of his gifts he noted with pleasure that, judging by its rather battered condition, was in constant use.

'It's our favourite book, Papa. And Emily coloured all the pictures, aren't they nice? Emily's very good at drawing too.'

As paintings of flowers were also shyly produced for his inspection, he put his arm around her and Rose said, 'I wish I was good at painting. Isn't she clever?'

'She is indeed,' said Faro, wondering where this new talent had sprung from. 'What shall I read to you?'

'King Lear and his horrid daughters,' said Rose quickly.

Faro suppressed a smile. Rose wasn't as sweet as she looked by any means, that sharp little mind held a taste for gore not unmixed by drama. She would perhaps grow up to be an actress, he thought, as she already knew pieces from Shakespeare she could recite by heart.

Actors had to have a sense of drama, an essential, too, in other professions. Politicians had it, so too had the clergy. And as he dutifully knelt down beside them while they recited the Lord's Prayer, his mind flew back to Balfray church earlier that day, remembering Reverend Erlandson and his sermon. He smiled faintly. Given an old man's wig, the minister could even have risen to King Lear, the part would have suited him well.

Faro slept without dreams that night and awoke to hear the sounds of a table being laid and appetising cooking smells issuing from downstairs. He was in time to walk his two daughters along to the school, enjoying the unaccustomed role of proud father meeting all their special chums and being shown off to their teacher, whom he doubted would last long at the school. She was too pretty by far, he thought appreciatively, not to be snapped up by some eager young bachelor.

Goodbyes said, hugs exchanged, with promises to see them again soon, he watched them out of sight, carried away in the midst of their friends. He waited at the gate's railings, hoping for a final wave, but he was already forgotten, and with him that family world they had briefly touched together. Turning away with a sigh, he decided it was better so. Knowing they were happy made separation easier.

Maybe he made too much of his own guilt as a father and he felt strangely reassured that Rose and Emily were well and happy, content with a loving grandmother and Aunty Griz. Far better off, he told himself, than they would be in Edinburgh with his uncertain life, its constant dangers.

And danger reminded him sharply of the reason for his visit to Orkney. Walking back down the road to the Procurator Fiscal's office he was told that the Fiscal had not returned but was assured that Sergeant Frith's message would be given to him immediately when he did. With that Faro had to be satisfied. He was not in all truth disappointed, sure that he was well on the way to unmasking the Balfray murderer. But there were a few ends left to tie together, a few enquiries to make with Vince's help, for that signing of the death certificate put his stepson's future in jeopardy.

Clearing Vince of any suggestion of negligence was one of Faro's main anxieties and he hoped fervently that in the next few hours they might put together the final fragments of the pattern before officialdom took over. Thoughtfully he walked back to the cottage and, on the off-chance that Aunty Griz was acquainted with everyone in Kirkwall, or by repute on Balfray, he determined to enquire about the maid Letty.

He found Aunty Griz wringing her hands, looking shocked and horrified. 'I've just heard about that poor crazed laddie doing away with himself. Awful, it is, awful, so soon after poor Mrs Balfray.' Stopping, she gave him one of her shrewd glances. 'I suppose that's why you're here really, isn't it?'

Faro smiled wryly. News travelled fast in the islands as it had always done best, by word of mouth – far faster than the newfangled telegraph could transmit or the newspapers could print. At least there were no details, he soon gathered, for which he was thankful.

Suicide was presumed and, nodding in agreement, he let her believe what she had heard. 'I believe he has a young cousin Letty who used to be maid at the castle. Lives in Kirkwall now. Do you know her?'

'Well, of course I do. She's Mrs Groat now, lives just two streets away.'

'I wonder if I could have a word with her.'

'Go easy on the bad news, Jeremy, though she'll have heard by now, no doubt.' Aunty Griz smiled. 'She's in, what they like to call these days, an interesting condition. She gets easily upset, the poor lass,' and tapping her forehead added significantly, 'A bit simple. Runs in the family.'

'Indeed?' Faro tried to sound surprised.

'At this time of day you'll find her in the cathedral, she does a bit of cleaning there. She turned very religious, after her experience. Thinks she saw the devil in the guise of a seal man on Balfray before she left.'

Aunty Griz chuckled. 'An instant conversion and a quick marriage, not before time by my reckoning, to her sweetheart over here. So I suppose it did some good, because rumour was that young Joe was hard pressed by his parents not to have anything to do with that family. We all hope this bairn will be all right. At least Joe Groat is good healthy stock. There's a boat at noon on Mondays, are you catching it?'

'I hope so. But I'll drop into the newspaper office. Some things I want to look up when I'm here.'

Aunty Griz put on her shawl. 'I'll walk you there.'

'I know where it is.'

Aunty Griz smiled and insisted on showing him to the very door of *The Orcadian* offices as if he, a grown man, would lose his way if he wasn't personally escorted.

But on the way he realised that she had her own reasons which had nothing to do with his well-being. As they walked towards Victoria Street it was obvious that she had a lot of friends, all out with their baskets doing their morning shopping. And Aunty Griz was having the time of her life, more than eager to stop each one and, after a formal introduction, tell them all about her famous nephew.

The walk took considerably longer than the two minutes he had envisaged. Leaving her with a hug and a kiss, he extracted a promise that she would visit him in Edinburgh.

'Aye, I might well . . . some day.'

He smiled at this promise he knew she would never keep.

The old newspaper files were being read by one of the reporters at this moment, he was told, and as they were bound up in book form, he would need to come back again in half an hour. In that case, he would go and see Letty Groat.

Chapter Sixteen

In the rose-red cathedral of St Magnus, Faro once more stood in awe before the magnitude of man's creation in the name of Almighty God. Again, considering the hovels of the poor, hardly advanced in many instances from Dwarfie Ha', he marvelled at those medieval Orcadian builders who, with the most primitive of tools but with boundless imagination and tenacity, had placed stone upon stone, pillar upon pillar, gallery upon gallery. And, as garnish to it all, the final inspiration of a stained-glass rose window.

As he walked down the nave towards the altar, there was no mistaking the heavily pregnant young woman so carefully cleaning the brasses. 'Mrs Groat?'

She almost jumped in the air at his approach. 'Yes, who wants me? Who are you? Oh, you did give me a scare. A body can usually hear anyone walking down the aisle.'

Faro had forgotten that one of the first lessons he had learned as a detective was to walk noiselessly. He felt he owed her an apology. 'I'm from Balfray.'

'Balfray?' she said, and he saw the fleeting terror in her face, the way she clutched the brass crucifix as if she meant to hurl it in his face. He took a step backwards at the violence of her action.

'Yes, I was bringing my children back to school in Kirkwall and . . . ' He paused, wondering how much she knew already. 'I thought I'd look in and see you.'

Mrs Groat sat down on the altar steps and began to

cry. Amazed once again at the speed with which news, especially bad news, travelled in the islands, he realised he would be spared telling her of her cousin's death.

'Poor Troller, poor Troller. Tell Saul, will you, that I can't come to the funeral wake. I know it's dreadful wicked of me but Joe will be going. I never want to set foot on that evil place, not ever again.'

'Why, what happened?' he asked innocently.

'I nearly died of fright, that's what.' She touched her stomach gently as if she felt the child moving. 'And . . . and . . . well, the bairn, you know.'

With a feeling that obtaining coherent information was going to be difficult, he asked, 'Do you mean when the housekeeper was drowned?'

She nodded. 'So they told you about it, did they? I asked them not to tell anyone, in case it got around and the selkies got after me too.'

Faro smiled gently. 'You should be safe enough here.'

'There's no place they can't get at you, mister.' She looked around wildly. 'And in any disguise too. That Inga, she's one. She's a witch,' she added viciously and then shook her head. 'But she's not all wicked, like some. She persuaded me to leave . . . '

'For your own good I'm sure, Mrs Groat.' And, trying to get her back to the main concern, he added, 'I'm making some enquiries about Mrs Bliss regarding relatives and so forth. I was hoping you could tell me exactly what happened, in your own words.'

Mrs Groat launched into the story of the seal man rising from the waves around the rock and snatching Mrs Bliss and her little dog into the sea. It was an unfaltering repetition of the version he had already been told at Balfray, in almost identical words.

He was disappointed. In that oft-repeated tale, fear had destroyed and distorted long ago any significant detail or relevant clues that a vital eye-witness account of Mrs Bliss's death might have originally contained.

Thanking her politely, he returned down the nave, stopping occasionally to look at the seventeenth-century tombstones – melancholy with ornate skulls and crossbones. Once the burial place of select Orkney families, it offered a gratifying sense of the continuity of man under one great roof. A story seven hundred years old, a harvest of times gone and dynasties long turned to dust.

At the massive doorway, he paused, looked back once more. Remarkable. Even the heathen, he thought, must be inspired and awe-struck, for the builders had also captured with the work of their hands, the peace which passeth all understanding.

Faro was not a man who troubled a busy God with his prayers except in moments of extremis, but here he felt the presence of a different deity to the wrathful Jehovah thundered out in two-hour-long sermons by preachers in fashionable Edinburgh churches. Here he felt, for one single instant, was the God of Love and he left wishing he had kept the simple faith of his childhood and envying those who had.

Stepping into the sunlight of Kirkwall on a busy Monday morning, he headed towards the offices of *The Orcadian* where, at the end of a long and tedious pursuit through the narrow news column files of the past months, he at last found what he was looking for.

Kirkwall Ferry Tragic Accident. Man Overboard

Captain Williams and his crew were summoned on deck by cries for help from a woman passenger, Mrs Leon, who, in great distress, informed them that she and her husband had been walking the deck to clear their heads. Mr Leon had felt suddenly unwell, having imbibed rather freely of ale at supper. As he leaned over the rail, and she assisted him, her hat, a new one bought for a wedding they were going to at Stromness, was caught by a sudden breeze. Mr Leon, trying to catch it, overbalanced and fell into the sea.

A witness to the accident, a Mr Brown, a business man from Aberdeen, confirmed that he had seen the couple walking together and had exchanged greetings with them minutes before the accident. He had noticed that Mr Leon was somewhat inebriated. Hearing Mrs Leon's cry of distress and witnessing her husband's gallant but useless attempt to save the hat, he had rushed to their assistance but, alas, too late to save Mr Leon.

Faro walked across to the police station, a tiny office manned by one constable. When he introduced himself, the policeman, who had hardly glanced up from reading the newspaper, sprang to his feet and saluted smartly.

'Sergeant Frith said we might be having a visit from you, Inspector. The Fiscal isn't back yet.'

'I know. I should like a glance at your log for the seventeenth February, if you please.'

The details were all there; a briefer account than that contained in *The Orcadian* simply stated, 'Mr G. Leon, from Banff, reported as falling overboard on Kirkwall ferry.' And in the adjoining column, 'Result of accident while drunk. No further details.'

'Was the body recovered?'

The Constable smiled pityingly. 'There are always bodies being washed up, Inspector. We have a fair number of wrecks around the coast, foreign ships as well as our own. But most of them are beyond identification by the time they come ashore.'

'Has Mrs Leon made any subsequent enquiry?'

'That I couldn't tell you, Inspector. Sergeant Frith's your man, deals with letters and so forth.'

'Very well. Will you please inform the Sergeant if

he has any relevant information that I am to be found at Balfray Castle. And tell him that it is a matter of urgency, will you?'

His next call was at the shipping office. He was in luck. The Kirkwall ferry was moored alongside and in reply to his question, the clerk answered, 'Captain Williams? Yes, sir, he's sitting over there.'

And Captain Williams, busily completing loading documents, cordially invited Inspector Faro to a seat. 'What can I do for you? Smuggling, is it?'

'No, not this time. Do you have a passenger list for February?'

The Captain shook his head. 'Anyone can buy a ticket. Depends on whether they booked a berth for the night crossing, otherwise we don't take names of passengers. However, if you'd care to come aboard, I'll have a look for you.'

Faro, following him up the gangway, said, 'It was the lady whose husband fell overboard last February that I'm interested in.'

'Oh dear, yes. The drunken gentleman. Most unfortunate, most unfortunate. Something about his wife's hat, wasn't it? No, I don't remember him, but I do remember the wife. Terrible state she was in,' he added, ushering Faro into his cabin. Taking down a ledger, he flicked back a few pages.

'February . . . you're in luck, Inspector. Here it is. A Mr and Mrs G. Leon were in Cabin Six.'

'I believe there was a witness, a Mr Brown, from Aberdeen?'

The Captain scanned the list and shook his head. 'No Mr Brown. He must have been a foot passenger.'

'Do you remember him at all?'

Captain Williams scratched his forehead. 'Only very vaguely that he was a well-spoken gentleman and very concerned for the poor lady.'

'May I see the list, please?'

One familiar name drew his attention. He pointed to it.

'Don't remember anything about that one,' said the Captain. 'Not that I'd want to. Bring bad luck. And this one certainly did. For someone.' Pausing, he added, 'What's this all about, anyway, Inspector?'

'Just insurance claims.'

'Insurance, eh?' The Captain eyed him doubtfully.

'Nothing you need concern yourself about, Captain.'

Faro left the ship with a sense of jubilation and a growing certainty that Mrs Leon did not exist. Soon he would have proof positive that she and Mrs Bliss were one and the same.

Walking down the gangway, he was acutely aware of the Captain watching him uneasily, confirming his own suspicion that Williams had been holding back, that he knew more than he was ready to admit. But what? He was soon to find the answer and from a totally unexpected quarter.

Heading along the quayside to discover that the Balfray mailboat would leave within the hour, he became aware of a prickling sensation in the region of the nape of his neck.

He was being followed. He knew now that his movements had been under close scrutiny since he left the ship. And before that, in the Captain's cabin, a lurking shadow had indicated a listener to their conversation. Turning a corner he leaned back against the wall. The footsteps grew closer.

'Got you,' he said, triumphantly seizing the seaman who had been tracking him in a vice-like grip from which there was little hope of escape. His captive wriggled frantically. 'Give over, mister. Give over. For God's sake. You're throttling me.'

Faro turned the man round. He recognised the grizzled weather-beaten face of the old sailor who had been sitting on a bench in the shipping office while he talked to Captain Williams. He released his merciless hold to be greeted by a bout of coughing and spluttering.

'God's sake, man, what are you? A prize fighter or something?' was the half-choked demand.

'Let's say that I don't enjoy being followed. I'm rather sensitive about such matters.'

'Let me go, mister.'

'I shall. When I know what is your business with me?'

'Nothing, mister. I was just curious when I heard you talking to the Captain. You see, I was on duty that night when that accident happened.' The man paused, fingering his throat tenderly. 'God, man, I could use a drink.'

'Very well.' And Faro led the way across to the Boat Inn where he set a jug of ale between them, the sight of which brightened the sailor's eyes and outlook so considerably that he volunteered his name was Henry.

'Drink up. Now what was it you wanted to tell me?'

'That night you was enquiring about when the woman's husband fell overboard. It wasn't just like the woman said. There was two men fighting . . . '

'Two men?'

'Aye, sir. And I got the feeling they was fighting over her. She was, well, cowering to one side. Looking scared.'

'Why then didn't you intervene?'

Henry laughed. 'Me? What do you take me for? Come between two men and their woman? Not likely. I've seen too many fights like that end up with the man in the middle coming off worst, with a knife sticking out of his back.' He shook his head. 'If I'd made a move, then I might have been the one to land in the drink.'

'Didn't you tell the Captain about this?'

'I'm coming to that, mister. I did tell him. But he told me it wasn't necessary to put that part into the report, especially when he had a witness report of the accident. All cut and dried.'

'Did you see this witness, Mr Brown, by any chance?'

Henry shook his head. 'I see what you're getting at, mister. You think he might have pushed the husband into the sea?'

'Never mind what I think, just answer my question, if you please.'

'No, I didn't see him. In any case I wouldn't have known him. It was a wild stormy night to start off with, heavy sea rolling and black as pitch.'

'But enough light for you to see two men fighting?'

'Aye, and hear them too. But they were all swathed up to the eyes, as any sensible body would be, walking the deck on such a night.'

'Have you any idea why the Captain didn't report this incident?'

'I can give a good guess. You see, it was his very first command and he didn't want trouble right at the beginning. I kept my peace too, but, if the body had been found and there had been an enquiry, then I swear to God, mister, I'd have come forward.'

Here indeed was a new dimension to Mr Leon's fatal accident. Two men involved and one woman.

'Remarkable,' said Faro and, handing Henry a gratuity, which was eagerly received, for his help, he leaped aboard the mailboat as it was casting off to Balfray.

Thankful that the crossing was a smooth one, for he needed all his wits about him to mull over some very interesting conclusions that had emerged from his enquiries, he was certain that the key to the labyrinth was almost within his grasp.

At Balfray, he skirted the castle drive and approached by the sea wood.

Was it only a sense of duty that led him to Saul Hoy's cottage, he wondered, where he was momentarily gratified to find Inga rolling pastry at the kitchen table, apparently none the worse for her attack on the cliff path.

When she saw him, he realised her face turned pale, her hands momentarily tightened. Then it was over. What dire news did she expect him to bring? It was obviously more than an anxious query about her health.

'I'm fine, just fine, Jeremy,' she said, clearly relieved.

'That bump on your head?'

'Getting smaller every hour.' She smiled. 'Won't you sit down and I'll make you a cup of tea?'

'No, thank you, I have to get back to the castle.'

'Surely it isn't all that urgent?' she pleaded.

'Some other time, Inga. I just wondered if you had any more idea who it was who attacked you yesterday.'

She shook her head, her eyes on the pastry-cutting. 'No idea at all, I'm afraid.'

'You don't sound very concerned.'

She looked up at him. 'I'm not.' With a shrug, she added, 'I bear a charmed life. Haven't you realised?'

'I shouldn't have thought yesterday afternoon's events were an indication of a charmed life,' he said grimly.

Smiling still, she shook her head. 'What you don't seem to realise, Jeremy, is that this was not the first time, or probably the last.' Enumerating on her fingers, she said, 'I've been stoned, tripped, cajoled and threatened. It's been going on as long as I can remember.'

'Then, for God's sake, why don't you take the warning and leave this place?'

She straightened up, put her hands on the table and leaned towards him. 'Is there something you want to ask me?' she whispered.

'Had you something in mind?'

'I thought you might be about to propose.'

His shocked expression told her that he was taken aback and with a sigh she added, 'I seem to be wrong, don't I?'

Gathering up the pie dishes, she said, 'I'm sorry. Now I've embarrassed you. I didn't mean to. Are you sure you won't have some tea?' And with a return to impish humour, she added, 'I can recommend tea. It's an excellent remedy for shock.'

Faro leaped to his feet, and said brusquely, 'I must go, really.'

'Very well. If you must.'

He waited until she closed the oven, wishing he could bring himself to stretch out his hand and touch her. At the door, he turned and, without looking at her, asked, 'What would your answer have been, Inga St Ola?'

'Same as before, Jeremy Faro. You had my answer twenty years ago. I haven't changed,' she said cheerfully.

But as she spoke she evaded his eyes and he was sure she lied, a bitter tight line about a mouth that smiled. He nodded and turned away. There was nothing between them now and he could return to Edinburgh untroubled, unfettered by any longing for Inga St Ola. He told himself that he was glad that he was not in love with her and had not been for many years, thankful that he need not tell her the truth.

As he walked up the drive to the castle, he was totally unprepared for the next disaster.

As he rang the doorbell, Vince rushed into the hall to greet him. 'Thank God it's you. Come quickly, Stepfather.'

'Is it Francis?'

'Yes. He's been poisoned.'

'Poisoned?'

And Faro swore as all his precious theories fell to dust.

Chapter Seventeen

'I hope you're handy with a stomach pump,' said Vince as they raced upstairs. 'Because, if we don't take action immediately, Francis is a dead man.'

The next hour was one Faro hoped never again to experience. Although insensitivity about gore was part of a policeman's life, it rarely had to do with the living and as they fought to keep Francis Balfray alive, Faro was thankful that he had never chosen medicine as a career. At last it was over and Balfray, drained and white, lay death-like against the pillows.

'I'll stay with him,' whispered Vince, pulling up the bedclothes.

'And I'll keep you company.'

'Good. When is the Procurator Fiscal coming?'

'As soon as he returns from South Ronaldsay and gets the Sergeant's message. Apparently they are like us here at Balfray, completely isolated without any telegraph system.'

'All very commendable unless you have an emergency. What happened in Kirkwall?'

Faro finished his account of the morning's events by sitting back in his chair, placing his fingertips together and regarding his stepson with a look of eager expectation.

'I have left out nothing of importance, Vince. You are now in possession of all the facts, so may I ask what you have deduced so far?'

Vince thought before replying. 'I would be prepared on your evidence to hazard a guess that Mrs Bliss and Mrs Leon are one and the same person.'

'Excellent.' And from his pocket, Faro produced the cipher which he had found in Mrs Bliss's notebook. 'We have it there, "Leon" in her own words. And what else?' he demanded sharply.

'I should like to know who her husband was, and where he fits into what looks undoubtedly like a conspiracy of some kind and why she was travelling under an assumed name.'

'Ah, Vince, Vince, you've missed the vital point. Take another look at these words she wrote— '

At that moment they were interrupted by Faro's mother who had been kept at bay with a story about Dr Francis having a severe gastric attack.

'It's almost dark and you haven't lit the lamps,' she said accusingly. 'You have hardly eaten a thing all day, Vince, and your stepfather hasn't had his supper yet.'

Vince smiled. 'I had forgotten, Grandma. But now that you mention it, I'm rather hungry.'

'I'll stay with Francis. Something on a tray will do excellently for me, Mother. Really it will,' Faro said firmly, silencing her protest.

While they were gone, Faro made some more notes. When Vince returned he was eager to discuss his deductions, but they had no sooner settled down at the table, heads together, when Francis opened his eyes.

'Why didn't you let me go?' he groaned as Vince bent over him taking his pulse.

'Be silent, Francis. Is that all the thanks we get for saving your life?'

Francis stared past him and, observing Faro for the first time, he said, 'You had better tell him, Inspector Faro.'

'Tell him what, Francis?'

'You have only saved me for the gallows.' Then with

a sigh he added, 'I killed her, Mr Faro. I killed my poor Thora.'

'Of course you didn't,' said Vince. 'It wasn't your fault she died. No one could have looked after her better. So please don't exert yourself. Talking wastes your strength.'

Francis shook his head and attempted to sit up feebly against the pillows. 'But I must tell you, if only to ease my terrible anguish. I have hardly slept since it happened.'

Disjointedly, with many outbursts of groans and tears, he began, 'It was Norma I loved and Norma I intended to marry. But when I came to Balfray I realised that the future of the island was at stake. Norma – Miss Balfray – was penniless.

'As for the Bothwell treasure, that was a legend only. There was no hidden hoard of gold. Whatever remained of that by the beginning of this century had been spent by her father and grandfather to build Balfray Castle and ensure better living conditions and houses for the tenants. Thanks to those two philanthropic relatives, she owned only the estate, heavily entailed, and it would soon have to be sold.'

He sighed. 'I could not bear the thought of Balfray falling into the hands of strangers. There was not a day from when I first came here as a child that I would not have made any sacrifice to possess it.

'As I expect you know, I came from a cadet branch of the family, but every man has his dream and when Sir Joseph befriended me, treated me as his son and put me through medical college, I knew that some day Balfray and Norma would be mine.

'And now I was faced with the terrible truth. I had come home to claim a bride and with her my heart's desire only to learn that we were in penury, and we would have to leave the island, seek another home.

'The thought was unbearable. I swore that I would do anything – anything – to keep Balfray. I think I was a little mad but I soon realised that the only way to save Balfray was through Thora. Thora had expectations. She came from a wealthy family on the distaff side and her mother had left her a considerable heiress in her own right.

'She also had the Balfray emeralds, which were of such value that possession of them alone would see the end of all our troubles. Besides, they were rightly Norma's and should have come to her if her besotted father hadn't willed them to his second wife, Thora's mother.

'Norma told me quite calmly there was only one way to save Balfray and that was for me to marry Thora. I wouldn't hear of it at first – marry for money? – but we both knew it was the only way, especially as Thora had already shown a considerable fondness for me.

' "You'll be able to persuade her to do anything for you," Norma told me. "And, after all, once she is your wife, the Balfray emeralds will also be yours. As for me, I will always be yours. Married to Thora or not, between us nothing is changed. You are still mine." '

Francis gave a shiver of distaste and looked at them pleadingly. 'I prefer not to dwell on those next few weeks, gentlemen, while I persuaded Thora that it was she I loved and wanted to marry, while she cried and told me how much she loved me, but how could she marry me and take me from her dear half-sister?

'Norma, however, was equal to the occasion, and, indeed, showed herself a greater actress than I had imagined. She told Thora that she had changed her mind, she no longer loved me or wished to be my wife.

'And so Thora and I were married. But I was bitterly unhappy with this charade I had embarked on.

I loved Norma and my sole consolation was having her live under the same roof. I am ashamed to say that . . . that she became my mistress very soon after I was a bridegroom.

'I was utterly captivated by her and I regret to say, gentlemen, that I was naïve enough to believe this curious ménage à trois might continue indefinitely. However, Norma became impatient. She made it clear that I had married Thora for one purpose only: to get possession of the emeralds and pay off Balfray's debts.

'She became a little less loving, a little less accessible and when, tortured by her neglect, I accused her of no longer caring about me, she indicated that the solution of the problem lay with me. That Thora was all that stood between us and a lifetime's happiness.

'The present position of deception and betrayal was odious to me. I wanted to make a clean break but when I suggested that I should divorce my wife, I realised with considerable horror that Norma had . . . had . . . a more permanent arrangement in mind.

'I refused even to discuss it. She did not argue and I believed that I had convinced her that I would never be party to what she had in mind. She seemed contrite and ready to abide by my decision that no harm should come to Thora.'

He paused for a moment, took a sip of water and then continued. 'It was soon after this that Thora took ill. She had a miscarriage in the early stages of pregnancy and I believed that it was through disappointment and depression that she failed to regain her strength.

'Now, gentlemen, mark the ways of fate. It was through losing our child that a bond was formed between us. And during that long illness, so bravely borne, compassion and tenderness for my little invalid turned into something else.'

He looked at them sadly. 'I fell in love with my own

wife. But this seemed in no way to dismay Norma. I expected, dear God I know not what, in the way of recriminations, but then I learned that her friendship with the new minister had developed by leaps and bounds. He had asked her to marry him and she had accepted.

'My delight was short-lived when she said that she still loved me. "This step is merely face-saving, for our reputations. It will also make our future plans easier for us to accomplish."

'Even then I failed to realise her monstrous intentions. When I discovered her with Erlandson in somewhat compromising circumstances, I was shocked but not totally displeased.'

He smiled wryly. 'A little disappointed, my manly pride injured, but I accepted the situation with relief. When she came to my room that night, I confronted her with her deception and she said, "The game's up, is that it, Francis?" It was then I learned what I can hardly bear to know even now, for she had long helped me in the dispensary. Now she told me that the laudanum-based tonic I was making up for my poor wife had been treated with arsenic. I knew then that it was too late to save her. But, if Balfray and I were to survive, I had to find a doctor to sign the death certificate. Preferably one who would never doubt my integrity.'

Pausing, he held out an imploring hand to Vince. 'It was then, I'm ashamed to say, I thought of you. I beg your forgiveness, old friend, for involving you in my sordid crime.'

Vince, tight-lipped, merely nodded and gave him another sip of water. Exhausted, he lay back against the pillows. But confessions were not quite at an end.

'The night before you arrived, Vince, it was Thora's turn. The Balfray emeralds were worthless imitations, she told me. The real ones had been sold long ago to pay off her grandfather's debts. Was that not a superb piece of irony, gentlemen? Surely you can understand that I cannot face the prospect of living any longer in this cursed cruel world.'

'A world of his own making, right enough,' murmured Faro, watching as Vince gave him a sleeping draught.

'I must go to Kirkwall with the tide, Stepfather,' he whispered. 'If he is to survive I cannot await fresh medical supplies arriving from Aberdeen. I must beg or borrow from the local doctor. You needn't stay, he'll sleep for several hours with the dose I've just given him.'

' "Oh what a tangled web we weave when first we practise to deceive," ' said Faro looking down at Francis Balfray. 'Aye, Sir Walter Scott's Marmion never said truer words than those.'

And, flexing his shoulders wearily, 'Norma Balfray's the guilty one, right enough, but no one can ever prove that she murdered her stepsister.'

'Unless she confesses, Stepfather.'

'I don't think we should set any store by that miracle, do you, lad?'

Vince shook his head. 'Whatever happens, she only set the wheels in motion, and poor Francis would have a hard time proving his innocence in a court of law since it was he, and he alone, who administered the fatal doses. He will always believe he was her murderer.'

'We can remove Francis from our list of suspects for Mrs Bliss and Troller Jack,' said Faro. 'But we must be vigilant. We still have to solve their murders. And let us not forget that a killer is still at large on Balfray. Perhaps waiting, at this moment, for the opportunity to claim another victim,' he added grimly.

Chapter Eighteen

'Miss Balfray?' said his mother. 'She went out ages ago. No, she didn't say where she was going and it wasn't my place to ask.' She looked at him curiously. 'She had a bag packed, like she was going off somewhere . . . '

Faro needed no further explanation. At the quayside, the Kirkwall boat was about to leave with Vince on board.

'No, Stepfather, she isn't here.'

So she must still be on the island. Wherever she was, if his suspicions were true, she was also in mortal danger. But where to begin his search?

As Faro stood on the cliff path, some instinct led him towards the Balfray vault. He was in luck. There was a flickering light inside, and voices raised in accusation. He moved soundlessly down the shallow steps, a perfect vantage point for observing, overhearing yet remaining concealed, for the gleam of the lantern on the floor effectively blocked any light from penetrating to the outside of the vault.

'Very well, you have been very ready with splendid excuses and explanations in the past, so perhaps you'll tell me what you intend doing now.' The speaker was Norma Balfray.

'Isn't it obvious, my dear?' Faro hardly recognised the man's real voice. 'What does a packed case suggest to you?'

'You're leaving Balfray, is that it? To start a new life – is that why you've shaved off your beard?'

'It is, indeed.'

'But the boat has gone. You can't go tonight.'

He heard the man's laugh, coarse now without any restraint. 'Think again, my dear.'

'The boat moored by Troll's Cave . . . '

'Of course. You imagined it was for pleasure but there was a much stronger reason. Emergency, my dear, an emergency just like this.'

'Take me with you . . . please. I can't live here without you!' He heard her despair as she cajoled, 'You promised. You did. Always.'

'Promises, what are promises when the game is up? Or it will be for me, as soon as the Fiscal gets here. Alas, I cannot afford meeting that gentleman face to face. We have older scores than Balfray to settle. And I'm afraid you will have to face whatever music is drummed up . . . for both of us. A sign of your love for me.'

'But what about the gold . . . the treasure we were to share?' she wailed.

'You were wrong about the Bee stone.' The lantern was raised, illuminating the niche where Thora Balfray now rested once more in her coffin. 'There is nothing but an empty hollow there now. The Bothwell treasure, if it ever existed, must have been spent long since. And I should have guessed, long before Thora confided in you, that those emeralds were paste.'

He laughed harshly. 'All this time wasted waiting for the right opportunity, for Thora to die so that the crypt would be reopened . . . '

'I helped you. Pretending to be in love with Francis, so that he would never suspect.'

'Waiting for Thora to die so slowly, a little each day, was an intolerable waste of my time. And to what end? I don't need to remind you of the disasters. You promised to help me then, but I had to do it alone. And when Troller came upon me, the game was up and I had to kill him. I thought he would be dead with the fall into the sea but I had to finish him off with the grave digger's spade. Very crude, my dear, not my style at all. Where were you when I needed you most?'

'I couldn't get away . . . '

'You couldn't get away! What a feeble excuse. You were afraid, weren't you? Terrified of your stepsister's ghost haunting her murderer . . . '

'Don't say that. Don't say it. Let us get away from here and I'll do anything, anything you say.'

'Too late for that, my dear. I have other plans.'

'Take me with you. I can do anything Mrs Bliss did.'

'But not so efficiently. We had been together for a long time, she was the perfect partner in crime.' He sighed regretfully. 'She was always a jealous woman, though. That was her only true weakness and, if she hadn't found out about us and in a fit of spite, turned informer, she would still be alive. I was a fool, I should have been more discreet.'

'You never really wanted me, did you?' Norma wailed. 'Oh, I see that now. I was just part of the plan to help you find the gold hoard.'

'What else, my dear? What else could you have ever hoped to be?'

'There's nothing at Balfray now. Just take me with you, that's all I ask.'

'Oh, I have no intention of leaving you . . . ' And as he drew the revolver out of his pocket Faro guessed his intention. Instinctively, hoping to save Norma, he dived forward.

His action dislodged a loose stone, which fell, crashing down the steps. Even as Faro lost his balance, Norma's lover leaped out and dragged him into the crypt.

'So we meet again, Inspector Faro. And for the last time.' He smiled, holding Faro at bay with the revolver pointed at his heart. 'This is one final parting I shall rather enjoy. I have looked forward to it for a long time now. I had not hoped to see you again so soon.'

'And in your true colours this time.' But, even as Faro said the words, he saw in the lantern light how the face before him, beardless now, could be the face he had been searching for in its many disguises.

'Noblesse Oblige, is it not?'

The man bowed. 'The same.'

'What is all this?' demanded Norma who had rushed to the man's assistance, clinging to his arm.

Faro recognised that in a straight fight, he could expect no help from her. But he could try. 'This man, Miss Balfray, to whom you have allied yourself, is a desperate criminal, one whom I have been pursuing over half of Scotland for months now. He is a robber and was a murderer, too, long before you set eyes upon him – I was trying to save your life,' he added in exasperation, for she refused to recognise her deadly danger.

'I don't believe it. You're lying.'

'Hear me out. This may be your only chance to hear the truth. He sent his accomplice Mrs Bliss to the island when he heard about the Balfray emeralds and the wealthy heiress. He also had a hoard of his own to keep hidden until the hunt was called off.'

Faro pointed with his foot to the case. 'If you lift that, Miss Balfray, you'll find it extremely heavy, weighed down with the proceeds of many burglaries – and murders, if you like. The law had almost caught up with him, we were close on his heels at Aberdeen and he needed a place to hide.

'His partner, Mrs Bliss, was already on Balfray, lured by rumours of an ancient treasure. By a stroke of fortune, she heard that a newcomer was expected. Under the name of Mr and Mrs Leon they met him on the ferry at Aberdeen, and disposed of him, by pushing him overboard. This cruel man you have allied yourself to then took his place . . . '

'I don't believe this. You're lying . . . '

'It was in the newspaper how a lady passenger saw her husband fall overboard, all the details are there. You must have read it on Balfray, surely?'

He saw by her look of amazement that he was right. 'Tell me it isn't true. Tell me the Inspector is lying.'

The man ignored her plea and snarled at Faro. 'You've been very clever, haven't you? Unfortunately I have now decided to tear myself away from Balfray and, alas, neither of you will ever live to give evidence. You were wrong about the boat too, Norma, as you have been about almost everything so far. There is a boat for me, but it's coming from France and it should be here before midnight . . . '

'I won't let you leave without me . . . I won't . . . You can't treat me like this . . . ' Angrily she pummelled him with her fists. Smiling, he pressed her briefly to his heart, like a forgiving lover.

She screamed. Just once.

Without moving, he fired a second time at Faro but the bullet went wide and the explosion reverberated through the vault.

Even as Norma Balfray slumped lifeless to the ground, the walls around them trembled and stones released themselves from their ancient moorings as the vault began slowly to disintegrate.

The man who was known as Noblesse Oblige dashed up the steps, turned and fired again at Faro. He missed, fighting for balance as the ground beneath their feet shuddered and began to slide fast, ever faster, towards the cliff top with a noise like the end of the world.

Faro reached his adversary, clung to his ankles, as past them both hurtled tombstones and coffins burst open to reveal the long and ancient dead. Shrouds twisted through the air, like faded grey ribbons, but still part of the nightmare, Faro kept his vice-like grip on his adversary.

Another explosion, close by this time. And in that moment before the world went dark, Faro realised he had been hit and that this was his death wound. He was dying. His last coherent thought was that it was both ironic and singularly appropriate that he should die in a straight fight with an old adversary. And in Orkney, too, the land of his birth.

As he hurtled through space, he saw his past rolling away down the centuries and becoming one with the dragon-headed Viking ships that had brought his first ancestors to set foot on this land. A bird's white wing curved, gleaming far above his head with exquisite beauty and, to the seals' cry as requiem, he was one with the dark and utter stillness of eternity.

It was Vince who clawed through the rubble by the shore, Vince who found him caught, held fast by a dislodged tree only a few yards from the top of the cliff. It was Vince who refused to believe that this cold bloody body was his stepfather's and that he could be dead, that there wasn't a flicker of life in him. It was Vince who listened, told himself that he detected a faint pulse and had him raised to the cliff top on an improvised stretcher.

It was to the sight of Vince that Faro's eyelids fluttered open. The black of endless night had given place to the endless white expanse of a large bed in Balfray Castle. 'Am I really alive? I thought I was dead.'

'You're a bit battered, Stepfather, but knowing you, you'll live to fight another day. But not tomorrow or the next day, that's for sure.'

There were other figures moving in the background of his new awakening. His mother, torn between tears and prayers, sobbing loudly. There was Inga, looking grave, in deep conversation with Sergeant Frith and a stranger in a top hat and frock coat.

'The Procurator Fiscal. He arrived ten minutes ago and I've given him the full report.' Leaning over, Vince took his stepfather's hand. 'Quite a day for him. And for the Sergeant. Francis is dead. Your mother stayed with him but then he said he was much better, hungry too, could she get him a bite to eat? Only too eager to oblige, when she came back, he'd taken an overdose of laudanum. It was the way he wanted it, Stepfather.'

'Poor Francis.'

'Poor island. It'll be put on the market, although I can't imagine anyone wanting to buy it. All things considered, don't you think we should let them all go in peace, Stepfather?'

'Are you asking me to compound a felony, lad, because in my weakened state I might agree, seeing that the three main participants are dead.'

Vince nodded. 'We found Norma's body. So she paid for her part in poisoning Thora.'

'And Francis paid for his.' Faro sighed, then continued. 'As for poor Troller, he made the mistake of coming to the crypt at the wrong moment. Moving Thora's coffin single-handed was impossible, the body would have to be removed first. But Norma lost her nerve for that particular operation. So when Troller surprised her lover, he couldn't be allowed to live . . . '

A shadow moved into the light, smiled at Faro and saluted him smartly.

'Captain Gibb led the search party,' said Vince. 'Weak heart or not, he did spartan work.'

'The old sea-dog – and my prime suspect,' said Faro. 'All he did was to have a real name from the letters of Noblesse Oblige they used for their various aliases. A piece of vanity that was ultimately to be their undoing although, I must confess, it led me well off the track.'

Vince smiled. 'But only temporarily. It wasn't until you showed me Erlandson's name on the passenger list that I got my first clue.'

'I got mine a little earlier. That amazing sermon. Epistle of Paul to the Romans, indeed, confused with King Lear. Do you know, Rose and Emily helped,' said Faro proudly. 'I remembered exactly where the quotations were from when I was reading them *Tales from Shakespeare*.'

'I still think it's amazing that he could sustain such a role and for such a long time.'

'Our Noblesse Oblige is no ordinary criminal. For one thing we know that he's a highly educated man – his appearance in the pulpit also confirms that. And the fact that he helped Captain Gibb with the Latin translations, that was the first time I had doubts whether the Captain was our man. It all fits in with what we know about our adversary, son of some noble house, who went to university and studied classics. Perhaps even divinity. Another fallen Lucifer, who knows?'

Faro paused, momentarily out of breath.

'You're talking too much. Take it easy, Stepfather. You can fill in the details later.'

Faro shook his head. 'What about him? Did you find his body too?'

Vince shook his head. 'No. Nowhere. He probably was not as lucky as you, his body carried out to sea. It was floodtide when we got there.'

'Floodtide. The cleanser of all evil.'

'Let's be thankful he's been washed away with all his sins. That's the last you'll see of that particular adversary, Stepfather.'

'No doubt.'

Vince looked at him sharply. For, despite his words, Faro sounded doubtful in the extreme.